"This man is dangerous and he's looking for you..."

"I'm coming," Faith insisted.

Something akin to admiration flashed in Eli's brown eyes before he nodded. "As you wish." He leaned inside and picked up the shotgun from where he'd placed it by the door. It would be just the two of them against a man who was highly trained and motivated by having everything to lose.

Grandmother Sarah took her hand. "Be careful. Both of you."

Faith forced a smile. "We'll be okay. Lock up behind us and don't open the door until we speak to you."

The fear in her grandmother's eyes hung heavily over Faith as the door closed. She hated the need to worry this precious woman, but the reality was Vincent had killed before. He wouldn't hesitate to take *Grossmammi*'s life if it benefited him.

He could be hiding in the woods, waiting for them to come to him.

Giving in to fear made her vulnerable to mistakes.

Faith couldn't afford a single wrong move if she wanted to live...

Mary Alford was inspired to become a writer after reading romantic suspense greats Victoria Holt and Phyllis A. Whitney. Soon, creating characters and throwing them into dangerous situations that tested their faith came naturally for Mary. In 2012 Mary entered the speed dating contest hosted by Love Inspired Suspense and later received "the call." Writing for Love Inspired Suspense has been a dream come true for Mary.

Books by Mary Alford

Love Inspired Suspense

Forgotten Past
Rocky Mountain Pursuit
Deadly Memories
Framed for Murder
Standoff at Midnight Mountain
Grave Peril
Amish Country Kidnapping
Amish Country Murder
Covert Amish Christmas
Shielding the Amish Witness

Visit the Author Profile page at Harlequin.com.

SHIELDING THE AMISH WITNESS

MARY ALFORD

LOVE INSPIRED SUSPENSE
INSPIRATIONAL ROMANCE

LOVE INSPIRED® SUSPENSE
INSPIRATIONAL ROMANCE

ISBN-13: 978-1-335-40514-2

Recycling programs
for this product may
not exist in your area.

Shielding the Amish Witness

Copyright © 2021 by Mary Eason

This edition published by arrangement with Harlequin Books S.A.

For questions and comments about the quality of this book, please contact us at CustomerService@Harlequin.com.

Love Inspired
22 Adelaide St. West, 40th Floor
Toronto, Ontario M5H 4E3, Canada
www.Harlequin.com

Printed in U.S.A.

This I recall to my mind,
therefore have I hope.
It is of the Lord's mercies that we are not consumed,
because his compassions fail not.
They are new every morning:
great is thy faithfulness.
            —*Lamentations* 3:21–23

To my granddaughter Ava, who never ceases to amaze me. You shine bright and make the world a better place. Love you so much, sweetie.

ONE

She'd put thousands of miles between herself and what happened, but she hadn't been able to erase the horrific memory of watching her friend die. It had played through her mind during every one of those miles, like a movie stuck on a never-ending loop.

All her fault. Cheryl was dead because of her.

The fear stalking her since she'd left New York showed no sign of easing as she crossed into Montana. Because she knew what Vincent was capable of. He'd proved it by killing his wife in cold blood without a single hint of remorse.

Faith had prayed that the terrible things she'd read in her late husband's note would turn out to be a cruel joke, but the rage on Vincent St. Clair's face when Cheryl confronted him with the evidence had annihilated that hope, and it confirmed he was the monster her husband wrote about. And so much more.

If you're reading this, then Vincent followed through with his threat and killed me...don't let him get away with it, Faith.

She swiped the back of her hand across her tired eyes and focused on the road in front of her. She was barely hanging on and still couldn't wrap her head around the truth. Vincent was Blake's older brother. Both were decorated police detectives. How was it possible they'd been on the take for years?

Since she'd found the note Blake had taped to the bottom of his desk, Faith had existed in a state of shock. The first person she'd thought to call was Cheryl.

Faith jerked the car onto the shoulder of the road and screamed into the confines of its interior. Pounded her fists against the steering wheel. If she hadn't been weak—hadn't called her friend for help—Cheryl would still be alive.

The horror of watching Vincent shoot his wife at point-blank range would forever be imprinted in Faith's mind. If Vincent had been ruthless enough to kill Cheryl simply because she'd seen the evidence Faith's husband had accumulated, then what would he do to Faith if he caught her? She'd grabbed the evidence and run, started the car and flown from the garage. She'd been so certain Vincent would shoot her dead right there, but God had protected her. She'd gotten away, but she'd been looking over her shoulder ever since.

"I'm so sorry." A broken sob escaped. Her heart drummed away the seconds while she glanced around at the isolation of the countryside and shivered. Sitting still was dangerous. Thirty-eight hours ago, she'd barely escaped with her life. But it wouldn't end there. Vincent knew she had evidence that would put him away for a long time. He'd follow her to the ends of the earth to silence her.

Faith eased the car back onto the road and punched the gas. Staying alive meant quickly getting the car out of sight. Vincent was aware of the type of vehicle she drove. He'd find a way to locate her. Every second she was out in the open, her life was in jeopardy.

Her gaze landed on the cell phone in the cup holder, and a terrible truth dawned. As a detective, Vincent would know how to track her phone. He could be following her now.

Faith grabbed the phone and powered it down, praying it wasn't too late.

She topped a hill. The snow flurries that had begun almost from the moment she crossed the state line continued to strengthen. An early spring storm was approaching.

Her fingers dug into the steering wheel as she drove through the deteriorating weather. More than anything, Faith hated bringing this nightmare to her sweet Amish grandmother. If there had been any other option, she would have chosen it instead.

A set of headlights struck the rearview mirror, momentarily blinding her. Faith whipped around in her seat. She hadn't seen a soul in hours. The wide-open territory surrounding the Amish community of West Kootenai was sparsely populated. There were few travelers. Especially after dark. Especially in this weather.

Her stomach plummeted. Was it Vincent?

You'll never get away from me... Vincent's parting words had felt more like an omen.

Tension bunched between her shoulder blades while she strained to see more details on the vehicle beyond the headlights.

As far as she knew, her husband and Cheryl were the only ones who had knowledge of her Amish past in Montana.

After she moved to New York, every time she mentioned once being Amish, she'd get asked dozens of questions about why she left. In the end, it was just easier to keep that part of her life secret.

Had either Cheryl or Blake mentioned her past to Vincent?

Please, God, no.

She picked up her speed while keeping close watch in the mirror. The vehicle topped the ridge behind her, its pace normal for the conditions.

She blew out a shaky breath, nerves shot. It was probably someone who had gotten trapped in the storm like her. Her grip relaxed on the wheel. She'd been jumping at shadows since leaving New York.

The car's headlights picked up the sign nailed to a tree by the side of the road announcing the different shops found in the West Kootenai community. Almost home. Just a little bit farther.

A wealth of childhood memories rushed through Faith's mind. For more than twenty years she'd longed to come back. With no other choice available, she believed God's hand had guided her throughout every mile of this frightening journey.

The Silver Creek Bridge appeared through the swirl of snow in her headlights. So many of her early childhood memories were tied to this creek. Her grandfather had taught her how to fish here. They'd searched for gold along the banks of the stream.

A smile played across her face at the way her *gross-daddi* could make anything seem like an adventure to a young child.

Tires squealed close and the sweet memories evaporated while goose bumps flew up her arms. A massive truck was a few feet off her bumper. She'd been wrong. This wasn't an innocent traveler. Her worst fear screamed out of her nightmares and into reality.

Vincent had found her. Staying alive was going to take all her skills.

He flipped his lights on bright to intimidate. Faith buried the accelerator and pushed the car to its limits. Her tires spun on the slick road. Even though it was springtime in other parts of the world, here in Big Sky Country, winter still had the community in its grip.

Silver Creek Bridge quickly came up. She had to cross it before he trapped her there.

Her tires connected with the first wooden slat on the bridge. From far too close on her bumper, Vincent revved his engine. Before there was time to have a clear thought, the truck plowed into her full force. Her car lurched forward. Faith's head flung toward the wheel then snapped backward.

She grabbed the door for support when another blow sent the full weight of her body slamming against her wrist. She screamed as pain shot up her arm. Keeping the car on the road with one working hand was difficult, but she wanted to live.

Her grandmother's home was past the bridge down the first gravel road on the right, but she didn't dare lead Vincent there. The next turnoff was several miles beyond. She'd never make it that far. If she drove the car cross country under these conditions, would she survive? Through the swatch of visibility the headlights created, much of the countryside appeared still covered in snow, and the storm was increasing.

Faith fought hard to right the car and keep it from slamming into the guardrail. She punched the gas and tried to put distance between herself and the vehicle that was inches off her bumper once more. The truck hit her again.

Her car spun sideways. Faith screamed and did her best to control the car, but Vincent didn't let up. He planted the truck's bumper against the side of her door and shoved. She watched in horror as the truck's tires coughed up smoke as he tried to force her off the bridge.

Faith yanked the wheel hard to the left in a futile attempt to pull free of the massive truck, but it was useless. Her car's engine was no match.

She stomped the brake pedal with both feet, but the car continued to inch closer to the guardrail.

The passenger side struck the railing. Metal grinding against metal sounded horrific as the car crumpled on impact. Vincent didn't let up. The guardrail bent under the pressure of the powerful truck. Faith fought a losing battle. Trapped inside the car there was nothing she could do to prevent it. She was going into Silver Creek.

Her terrified gaze shot to the water below. The creek was close to overflowing its banks and had to be five feet deep.

The railing gave way with a terrible sound of metal snapping and bolts breaking free. Both passenger tires left the bridge. The car hung suspended in midair for the time it took Faith to pull in a fearful breath. Vincent's gleeful expression would forever be imprinted in her memory. She teetered back and forth for a second longer then plunged into the icy waters of Silver Creek.

The noise of the impact was so horrendous it had her wondering if the car would break into a hundred pieces. Her injured wrist banged the door again. She screamed and blacked out for a second.

Freezing water poured in through the bottoms of the doors.

Faith fumbled with the seat belt latch. It didn't budge. *Not like this.* She wouldn't die trapped inside this vehicle. She'd fight with everything she had to live. Expose Vincent for the criminal he was.

Water continued to rise inside the car. It groaned under the shifting pressure.

"Help me. Please," she prayed and jabbed her finger against the latch several more times. The final try released the seat belt. She'd escaped her house with just the clothes on her back and the pieces of evidence she'd tucked inside her purse that would bring down Vincent. She wouldn't lose them now.

Faith grabbed her purse and phone before they were completely submerged. She shoved the phone inside the purse and closed it before she slung the strap over her head.

It was a blessing the car had manual window cranks because the water had shorted the electrical system.

Faith rolled down the driver's window and eased through the opening. Immediately, she sank under the water's surface and tried not to panic. Her feet touched the bottom, and she righted herself. Though her head was above the water, the creek was running swiftly and standing up against the current was nearly impossible.

The cold water took her breath away. From where she stood in the middle of the creek, the bank appeared miles away.

Keeping her eyes on land, she began walking. She'd

taken only a few steps when she stumbled on the rocky creek bed and went under the water.

Fighting back alarm, she steadied her feet beneath her. She wasn't a strong swimmer in the best of conditions, but she'd never make it to the shore like this. There was only one choice. She'd have to swim diagonally to reach dry ground.

One stroke at a time. Her grandfather had taught her that valuable lesson. When she was in the water, panicking was the worst possible enemy. Take each stroke and follow through. Keep your focus on your destination. She sucked in a breath, tried to calm herself and did as he'd taught her.

Where had Vincent gone? She scanned the bridge above. No truck. She hadn't heard it leave, but she'd been too focused on saving herself.

As the car begin to settle, a sharp crack came from the woods above and close to the road. She recognized the sound immediately from the many times Blake had taken her to the gun range. Gunfire. Vincent was shooting at her. He was determined she wasn't going to leave here alive.

More shots landed all around. Barrel flashes lit up the woods. Vincent scrambled down the embankment. The shots missed her by inches. Faith ducked beneath the surface to keep from being hit. She swam underwater until she reached the opposite side of the car.

"Did you really think you could get away? From me?" Vincent mocked. "There's no way I can let you live. Cheryl's dead at your house. I used Blake's weapon to kill her. You remember—the one he taught you to shoot with. Your fingerprints are all over it. By now, my police buddies have probably found her body.

I'll tell them you tried to kill me too. No one will blame me for taking you down."

Those ominous words threatened to destroy her. Vincent planned to frame her for Cheryl's death. Her murder would be considered justifiable by his fellow cops.

"Where's the evidence Blake left you?" Vincent demanded. "Give it to me and maybe I'll let you live."

There was no way she trusted him to keep his word. Once he had the evidence, he'd kill her.

Using the car as a barrier, she peeked around the edge. Vincent spotted her and opened fire. Faith ducked beneath the water. As she resurfaced, the purse slipped from her head and begun floating away. The clasp worked its way open. It wouldn't take long for everything inside to be in the creek.

Faith grabbed for it like the lifeline it was. That purse contained her only means of contacting anyone and the hard copies of all the data on the thumb drive along with Blake's note describing his and Vincent's crimes.

She'd tucked the drive into a plastic bag inside her wallet and placed it in her purse before she'd called Cheryl. At the time, she hadn't imagined a scenario such as this. God had planted the notion in her mind. If she lost those items, she had nothing.

Faith dove for the disappearing purse, but the current was too swift, and it floated out of her reach. Another round of shots peppered the water around her, forcing her to retreat. Desperate, she looked around for some means of escape, but there wasn't one. It was just her and a killer who was determined to bury her at the bottom of the creek. Along with his crimes.

* * *

Gunshots—more than one—had Eli Shetler sitting up straighter on the wagon. A short time earlier another disturbing sound had interrupted his tired thoughts. Metal crunching together followed by a loud splash. Something quite large had gone into Silver Creek. Undoubtedly, a car. But that didn't explain the gunshots. Those worried him the most.

Eli shook the reins hard. The mare picked up her pace.

The bridge over Silver Creek appeared through the snowy downpour.

Though he'd been back in West Kootenai for a little more than a month, everywhere he looked moments from his past abounded. Good times. Bad times. Those he and his wife, Miriam, had spent together reminded him of all he'd lost with her death. Silver Creek was no exception. They'd picnicked here. Taken long walks through the nearby woods to spend time together when they were courting. And he'd loved her so much. Even after two years, he couldn't believe he would never see her or the baby they'd been expecting again.

Eli stopped the horse before she entered the bridge. Part of the guardrail to the right was missing where a vehicle had plowed through it. The image in his head was unsettling.

A little way down on the opposite side, a pickup truck was parked off the gravel road. Had the driver stopped to lend assistance? While he pondered these things, a half dozen more shots ricocheted from the creek below. This was no accident. Someone was in serious trouble.

Eli grabbed the shotgun he kept for protection when

working out in the wilderness and started down the slippery embankment.

"Help!" A woman screamed at the top of her lungs. Her distressed voice sent Eli scrambling the rest of the way down.

As his eyes adjusted to the darkness below the bridge, the sight in front of him was like nothing he'd seen before. A woman was in the water near a car that was sinking quickly. On the bank nearby, a shadowy figure of a man. He had a gun aimed at the woman.

"Where is it?" the man demanded. "I want what Blake gave you. All of it. Now," the man barked, and the woman jumped in reaction. "You should have stayed out of this, Faith. Shouldn't have dragged Cheryl into it. Now, you're going to die like her and your traitor husband. He betrayed blood."

Eli was terrified the man would shoot her right before his eyes. Acting on sheer instinct, he charged toward the assailant.

The man whipped around, spotted Eli, and trained his weapon at his head.

"That's far enough." The man scowled as he looked Eli over without lowering the weapon. "This doesn't concern you. I'm a police officer." He reached inside his pocket and flashed a badge too quickly for Eli to read it. "This woman is being accused of murder. I'm here to take her back with me."

"He's lying!" the female yelled, her pleading eyes latching on to Eli. Something familiar about her startled him. "He tried to kill me by forcing me off the bridge. Now he's shooting at me."

The reality of those words sank in. Why would someone from law enforcement try to kill this woman?

Something about the situation wasn't as this guy claimed.

The man kept his finger poised on the trigger of the weapon. Would a law enforcement officer try to kill a man who had come to assist? Eli had overheard him threatening the woman earlier. The man might be a police officer, but he was definitely not following the law.

"Please don't leave me with him." The terror on her face wouldn't let Eli abandoned her no matter how much this man threatened.

"She's coming with me," Eli said and moved toward the woman.

"I told you to stay out of it. This is a police matter." He waded into the water and grabbed the woman's arm, yanking her along with him. "Let's go. It's a long drive back to New York."

"Stop right there." Eli raised his weapon. "Let her go." Though he was far from steady on the inside, Eli kept the shotgun trained on the man's midsection.

The officer shoved the woman away and strode toward Eli.

"Don't come any closer." Eli fired the shotgun into the air as a warning, yet the man didn't back down. He pointed the handgun at Eli and shot. If Eli hadn't ducked in time, the bullet would have struck his head. He couldn't believe stopping to lend a hand had resulted in a life-threatening situation.

Eli dove for the shooter before he could get off another round. They struggled in hand-to-hand combat while his assailant tried to get the handgun into a position to shoot again. Fighting for his life, Eli slugged the man. Watched him stumble backward before losing his footing on the slippery grass. He hit the ground hard.

Not giving his attacker time enough to right himself, Eli snatched the gun free from his grasp. Without a weapon, the man's threat was greatly diffused, yet he didn't appear ready to give up. He jumped to his feet, fists balled at his sides. With a look of pure malevolence on his face, he took a threatening step closer.

Eli cocked the handgun. "That's far enough. I don't want to shoot you, but I will."

His attacker stopped short, realizing Eli had the upper hand.

He glared long and hard before he dusted off his clothes. "This isn't over, and you're in a lot of trouble for interfering in a murder investigation."

The tingle along Eli's spine convinced him it was a lie. Given the opportunity, this man would take the weapon from him and use it on Eli and the woman standing in the creek. What kind of police officer would do such a thing?

"You need to leave." He kept the weapon leveled on the man's chest. "Now, before the sheriff arrives." Though Eli had no way of knowing if some of his *Englisch* neighbors had heard the shots and called the sheriff, it was a *gut* possibility. People around these parts looked out for each other. And he wanted this man to believe help was on the way.

"You didn't call anyone." But there was just enough doubt in his tone to make it clear he wasn't certain. "And even if you did, who do you think he'll believe. An Amish man and a woman accused of murder. Or a police detective."

Eli shook his head. "We will find out soon enough. One of my neighbors would have called in the gunshots by now. Unless you want to explain to the sheriff why you tried to kill me and ran this woman off the road, I suggest you be on your way."

The man hesitated for a long moment before he tossed the woman a venomous look. "I'll be back for you and the stuff." With that warning hanging over their heads, the man stormed past Eli and slammed his shoulder against him. Without another look their way, he stomped up the embankment and into the woods.

Reality crashed down around Eli. His knees threatened to buckle beneath his weight. He'd never been in a situation like this before. One minute he was on his way home after checking out the new piece of property he and Hunter planned to log, and the next he was interrupting a murder plot.

Near the road, the truck's engine fired, and the vehicle screamed away. The man had left…for now.

Eli snapped out of his shock and hurried to the woman who appeared to be suffering from her own form of trauma. She clutched her soaked jacket around her body and shivered. Once again, he was struck by a sense of familiarity. Did he know her? Impossible, surely.

"*Komm*, my wagon is up on the road, and I have some blankets you can use to dry off and warm up. It's best if we don't stay here any longer. I don't trust him not to come back." A loud whoosh snapped their attention to the water where the car slipped farther into its watery grave. Only the roof remained visible.

If he'd taken a different path home…

Eli suppressed a shiver.

"H-he forced me off the road. If you hadn't come along when you did, he would have killed me." Her teeth chattered from the cold, and she held her wrist against her body as if it had been injured in the incident.

"Is it true he's a police officer?" Eli asked because he had to know what he was dealing with.

She nodded. "It's true. But he's a dirty cop, and he knows I can prove it. That's why he tried to kill me. He's a dangerous man." She glanced up toward the road as if expecting the shooter to return.

"You're safe now." But for how long? Eli went to assist her, but she shrank away. Despite his coming to her aid, she didn't fully trust him yet. After what happened, he could certainly understand.

She pushed her dark hair away from her face and searched his. "I'm sorry. It's just… I was so sure he'd kill me." She blew out a sigh. "Thank you for rescuing me."

Eli found himself swept up into the turmoil burning inside her troubled green eyes, which held fear and suspicion. He wanted to understand what had happened here tonight because there was so much more to her story.

"You are welcome. My name is Eli Shetler." He introduced himself, hoping to put her at ease.

Surprise showed on her face. "Eli? I remember you," she said in amazement. "My name is Faith… Cooper."

Faith Cooper? His neighbor was Sarah Cooper. As he continued to stare at her, something about her appearance sparked the tiniest of memories. This was Sarah's *Englisch* granddaughter.

"Your *grossmammi* is Sarah Cooper, right?" He couldn't hide his shock as he realized the woman standing before him now was the grown-up version of that little girl who used to follow around her grandfather everywhere he went. The one who tagged along behind Eli whenever she could. He remembered the time when she and her parents had left the Amish faith.

Faith smiled at his surprise. "She is."

"I remember you." And he did. The sweet little dark-haired girl she'd once been. So curious about everything. How had someone like her gotten involved with a man who was trying to kill her?

"How do you know that man?" Eli asked. "He said you were wanted for murder?"

She pulled her gaze from his. "He's lying. He killed his wife who is—was—my best friend. He did it in front of me, and now he's trying to frame me for her death."

Her chilling words were hard to believe. The desire to ask more questions was hard to resist, but they both needed to get out of here before that man returned. "Those are serious accusations. Way beyond what we can handle ourselves. We need to get the sheriff involved."

She barely let him finish. "No. No police. He's a detective. The sheriff won't believe me over Vincent, and if the tables were turned, I probably wouldn't believe me either." She stumbled over the slick path as they headed up the embankment. Eli reached out to catch her before she fell. Once more, he noticed the way she kept her left wrist tucked close to her body. "You're hurt. That could be serious." He indicated her injured wrist. "At least let me drive you to the hospital in Eagle's Nest." Though the town was some ten miles away, it was the closest clinic to the community.

She shook her head. "No, it's too risky. The best thing I can do is get out of sight as quickly as possi-

ble. He may have left for now, but he won't give up."
She stopped as if she'd said too much. "And it is only
a sprain."

Eli kept his doubts to himself. Once they reached the
road, Eli helped her climb onto the wagon. He glanced
back at Silver Creek and tried not to think about what
might have happened if he'd worked a little longer.
Taken a different path home. *Gott* had been looking
out for her.

Grabbing blankets from underneath some of his
tools, Eli then wrapped one around her legs. The other
he placed over her shoulders.

Springtime in West Kootenai was deceptive. The
warmer temperatures lulled you into a false sense of
hope. And then a storm like this one happened.

He climbed up beside her, yet he did not attempt to
take up the reins. The questions pounding his mind
needed answering, but Faith appeared to be one more
bad thing away from falling apart.

So far, she hadn't said anything to settle his doubts.
Faith claimed this man coming after her was a dirty
cop who had killed someone. Was he involved in more
illegal activities? Was she?

*I'm a police officer. This woman is being accused
of murder.* The man's troubling words played through
Eli's mind again and again. Though he didn't believe
Faith was capable of murder, there was much about
what happened that he didn't understand.

He thought about the trouble following him for the
past two years. Losing his wife was hard enough but
being accused of setting the fire that caused her death
was unthinkable. He'd had firsthand experience with
being accused of something you didn't do.

Eli gathered the reins from where he'd slung them in haste.

"Thank you, Eli," she said and faced him. "I'm sorry I put you in the middle of this, but I'm truly grateful you stopped. I'd be dead by now if you hadn't, and I doubt if anyone would know about it."

Those alarming words confirmed the seriousness of what happened tonight.

"You and I were friends as *kinner*, and Sarah is my neighbor. I would do whatever I could to help either of you."

She smiled at his recollection. "You used to walk me home from school sometimes. I remember you always chose pretty rocks for me." Her smile disappeared. "It's been so many years ago since I left here. At times, it feels like another lifetime."

He certainly understood that feeling. He'd been gone from West Kootenai for a long time himself. The life he left behind was not the same one he possessed now. It would never be the same.

"Your *grossmammi* isn't expecting you, is she?"

She shook her head, confirming this wasn't a friendly visit to catch up. Faith was running for her life.

Eli gave the reins a shake, and the horse responded to his skilled direction.

"Why is this man trying to harm you? Why would he try to frame you for someone's murder?"

She put up her guard. "Because of the things I found out. It's better for him if I disappear." The answer didn't settle anything in Eli's mind. Far from it.

They passed by the damaged railing. Eli had a feeling the truth was going to be far worse than anything he could imagine.

The mare clomped along the slushy road while snow continued to fall. Eli kept a close eye behind them. The truck had headed away from the community, but something told him this wasn't the last they'd seen of the man.

Most people around the town and the surrounding countryside knew each other. Had grown up living with the same neighbors for several generations. A stranger would stand out. He'd ask some of his *Englisch* neighbors if they'd seen a stranger. Eli hoped the man would realize it was better off for him to go back to where he came from.

The turnoff to his and Sarah's homesteads appeared up on the right. At one time all the property on this side of the road was deeded to the Cooper family.

When he'd first come back to West Kootenai, he'd remembered the property that once belonged to Sarah's son was sitting vacant, so he'd asked to buy some of the land and the old house. She'd been more than agreeable.

Being reunited with his family again had come at a heavy price. If it weren't for his *fraa*'s passing, he wouldn't have come back. For more than ten years, his relationship with his brothers had been strained. After losing Miriam and their unborn child to the fire, living under suspicion had gotten to be too much. He'd wanted a fresh start. Eli had reached out to his *mamm* and found the welcoming he'd longed for. But he still felt it necessary to keep some distance between himself and the family. Maybe out of a sense of guilt for his part in what happened between himself and *Bruder* Mason.

And so, he'd bought the place next to Sarah's. It was some distance from the rest of the family and away from most of the community. He enjoyed the privacy and Sarah's calming presence.

Her modest homestead came into view. Eli guided the mare down her narrow drive and stopped in front of the house. Puffs of white smoke disappeared among the snowy night air.

He turned to Faith. Tears glistened in her eyes as she stared at the house, and he wondered when she'd been here last. He of all people understood how hard homecomings could be.

Eli hopped down and helped her from the wagon. In the distance an engine revved, and she spun at the sound.

"It could be coming from the highway. Sound travels far out here." Yet he understood exactly what she was thinking because he'd thought the same.

She relaxed. "You're probably right." Without another word, she hurried up the steps to the porch. Faith stood in front of the door for a long moment before she knocked.

Eli followed at a slower pace. He didn't have it in his heart to tell her the engine noise was much closer. After what happened at the creek, there was no way he was leaving two women alone with a killer on the loose in the community. He'd find a way to stay close. Sarah wouldn't have a problem with him bunking on the sofa.

Even though he'd been home for just over a month, he and Sarah had become *gut* friends. As a widow alone, she relied on him, and he was happy to help her out in any way he could.

A single lantern showed through the window. Sarah would be working on her quilting. The one thing she enjoyed most these days.

"Sometimes her hearing isn't so *gut*," Eli told her. "You have to knock louder."

Faith drew in a breath and knocked harder. Waited.

As he listened, the familiar labored steps of the woman who had welcomed him back to the community with open arms came toward them. The curtain near the door moved.

"Sarah, it's me, Eli. I have someone here to see you."

The curtain dropped and the door opened. A smile creased her face. Sarah's smile always made the darkness that haunted him flee.

"Eli, I'm glad you stopped by. *Komm* inside. The night is cold. I'll make some coffee to warm you up." Sarah's gaze shifted from him to the woman at his side. "And who is this?"

She stepped closer. Recognition dawned in slow surprise. "Faith." Tears quickly filled her eyes. "It is you." She swept her granddaughter into her arms and hugged her tightly. "Oh, my *boppli*. My precious *boppli*. You're finally home."

As much as Sarah was overjoyed to see her granddaughter, Eli worried that the danger following Faith would find its way into this gentle woman's life.

TWO

Faith clung to her grandmother and didn't want to let her go while tears she couldn't control continued to fall. Through all the years—the miles—the fears that shadowed her every bit of the way here—she was finally home. And no matter what Vincent threw at her, she needed to believe everything was going to be okay because she was in her grandmother's loving arms.

"I can't believe I'm finally here," she said with a watery smile. Faith clasped her grandmother's hand and together they stepped inside the house followed by Eli. He closed the door softly.

Childhood memories flew through her mind. Whenever she was scared or troubled by something, she'd come here and pour out her heart to this special woman. During this past year since Blake's death, after she'd found out her grandmother was still alive, her heart had been aching to come back home.

This was the first time she'd been back since her father moved the family away when Faith was ten. For a long time after they'd left, she'd begged her mother to let her write to the grandparents, but she'd said her father wouldn't approve. Several years later, her father told her both grandparents had died. Faith had cried for weeks after hearing the heartbreaking news before finally accepting the truth. At least what she'd thought was the truth until she'd realized her father had lied to her.

After Blake passed away, Faith found herself longing to return to the simple way of life she'd been forced to leave. A few weeks before she'd discovered Blake's note, she'd found the address for the bakery in West Kootenai and had written Mrs. Stoltzfus, the owner and her grandmother's good friend. Faith had wanted to visit her grandparents' graves and perhaps stop by their old homestead. When the response came, it just about floored her. Grandmother was still alive. Her father had lied to keep her from reaching out to her grandparents through the years. Faith and her grandmother had connected through letters. She'd planned a visit to West Kootenai soon, and then... Vincent had happened.

The familiar childhood scent of wood smoke and the lavender soap her grandmother made melted the years away. She was that little girl again. Running to her grandmother to make it better.

She became aware of Eli watching their exchange. Though the tears wouldn't stop, Faith was all smiles. This was the place she'd yearned to be for so long.

"I'm so happy to see you again," she told her grandmother.

Grandmother Sarah's keen brown eyes looked deeply into hers, seeing the things that Faith wasn't ready to talk about just yet.

How could she tell this sweet lady about the deadly

crimes her husband had been involved in when Faith couldn't reconcile them with the man she'd loved?

Her grandmother noticed the way Faith cradled her injured wrist. "You're hurt."

Faith dismissed her grandmother's concern. "It's only a sprain." She'd carefully examined the injured wrist during the ride over. Once she had it wrapped and a few weeks of healing, it would be better.

The heat from the woodstove called to her. She stepped closer. It warmed her chilled skin, yet she still couldn't stop shaking every time she pictured Vincent's angry face. She'd almost died tonight. Had been minutes from it before Eli came along.

"*Komm.* Sit." Grandmother Sarah gently urged her into one of the rockers. "You are soaking wet, child. What happened? How did you run into Eli?" Her eyes widened as they traveled over Faith's damp jeans, sweater and jacket. Faith's dark hair dripped water onto the floor. After more than a day without sleep and being forced into the creek, Faith couldn't imagine how bad she must look.

"I ran off the Silver Creek Bridge," she said in answer to her grandmother's probing gaze. "My car landed in the water." It wasn't the whole truth, but she didn't know where to begin to describe the horrible things Vincent had done.

Grandmother Sarah tsked and shook her head. "You could have been killed."

"Thankfully, Eli came along in time to save me." She glanced past her grandmother to where Eli leaned against the wall near the door. His intense eyes were watchful. Broad shouldered, his presence dominated the tiny living room. The lantern on the wall near him picked up hints of gold in his brown hair that touched the collar of his dark blue shirt. A neatly trimmed matching beard confirmed Eli was married. She hadn't realized the young boy who she once had a crush had wed. She felt guilty about keeping him from his wife.

"Thanks be to *Gott*," Grandmother Sarah exclaimed and turned to Eli. "*Denki*, for helping my precious granddaughter. You're a good boy." She patted the arm of the man who was far from a boy.

Eli shrugged off the thanks. "I did what anyone else would do." He met Faith's gaze and held it. "You should tell your *grossmammi* the truth. This involves her now."

Grandmother Sarah swung toward her. "What's he talking about?"

Faith pulled in a steadying breath. Forced out the words. "I didn't accidentally run off the road tonight. I was deliberately forced off by someone I know."

"Who would do such a thing?" For people like her grandmother and Eli, the thought of such evil existing had to be hard to fathom. The peaceful lifestyle of the Amish insulated them from the ugliness that sometimes took place in the *Englisch* world.

At one time, Faith had been just as innocent. Never imagining anything bad could happen. But that was before Blake's death. Before she knew the truth about her husband's and Vincent's crimes.

"Someone very bad." And it was true. Vincent was a bad man with everything to lose.

"With your permission, I would like to bunk here tonight." Eli spoke to her grandmother. After what happened, knowing Eli was close would help put Faith's mind at ease. Still, he wondered what she was keeping him from.

"Won't your wife be worried about you?" The words slipped out before Faith could stop them and a desolate look entered Eli's eyes.

"My wife is dead," he said in a voice devoid of emotion.

Faith wished for the floor to swallow her. "I'm so sorry."

While they continued to watch each other across the small space, Grandmother Sarah's troubled gaze turned to Eli. "You are always welcome here. I will make up the sofa for you. It will be *gut* to have you close."

A faint smile replaced the dark expression on his face. He and Grandmother were close.

"*Denki*, Sarah. I will put the mare in the barn and be right back," he said while holding Faith's gaze. She understood he was giving them time alone for Faith to tell her grandmother about Vincent. "Lock the door up behind me to be safe."

Eli grabbed his hat and the lantern, stepped outside and closed the door. Grandmother Sarah slid the lock into place and came back to where Faith sat.

She placed her hand on Faith's shoulder and nodded. "*Gut*, you are no longer shivering." Without another word, she brought over a towel then headed for the kitchen, but Faith grabbed her hand.

"Aren't you going to ask me why someone would want to run me off the road?"

Her grandmother smiled and kissed Faith's cheek. "You will tell me the whole story when you are ready."

Just like her grandmother. Growing up, whenever something was troubling Faith and she couldn't bring herself to share it, Grandmother Sarah would always wait until she was ready to talk. She never once forced the matter.

With a pat on her shoulder, Grandmother Sarah left her alone. Familiar sounds drifted from the kitchen while Faith stared at the fire in the woodstove. She could only think of what she'd left behind in Silver Creek. Though she didn't fully understand all the information on the thumb drive, one thing became apparent—Blake and Vincent were on the payroll of one of the biggest drug dealers in New York. A man Blake had referred to as Ghost.

Her husband had included detailed accounts of drug raids that had taken place with rival dealers. He'd mentioned amounts of money that had been confiscated along with the discrepancy to what got logged in. There were names of other cops listed, along with dollar amounts they'd been paid.

But something else that she'd seen on one of the pages had scared the daylights out of her. Names of people whose cause of death had been pinned on someone else. Blake claimed Vincent had handled all the murders.

"Here you are, my *boppli*. Drink up." Grandmother Sarah handed Faith a cup of hot chocolate like she used to make when Faith was a child.

"You remembered." Her heart melted with happiness, despite the danger still coming for her.

Grandmother Sarah beamed. "Of course, I remembered. You are my baby girl. I remember everything about you."

The guilt that had haunted her since she'd reconnected with her grandmother returned full force. She should have realized her father would do everything in his power to keep Faith away from her grandparents.

"I should have ignored *Daed*'s anger and checked on you and *Grossdaddi* sooner. I missed out on so many years of happiness with you both because of it."

Even though she'd been only ten at the time, Faith still remembered the argument between her father and *Grossdaddi*. The angry words her father had thrown at his *daed* before he packed up his family and moved them thousands of miles away.

Her grandmother patted her hand. "My *sohn* was a troubled boy. Saul hated this way of life. He always wanted more than what he could find here." She shook her head and got to her feet, then brought over gauze for wrapping Faith's injured wrist.

"How are you doing, really?" Faith asked when she noticed the way her grandmother rubbed her hands together as if to ease the pain.

"I am blessed." This was always the answer whenever Faith had asked about her health in letters. But her grandmother's gnarled hands were a reminder that she was getting older. Though Grandmother Sarah had joked about the cold making it hard to work on her quilts, Faith had no idea how bad her arthritis had become until now.

She couldn't change the past, but Faith could do everything in her power to never let down the one person who truly cared about her again.

Grandmother Sarah finished wrapping Faith's wrist and stood back to examine her work. "How does it feel?"

"Much improved. I couldn't have done it better. You were my inspiration for becoming a nurse, the way you always helped others." She squeezed her grand-mother's arm.

"*Komm* with me. I have an extra dress for you to change into." She followed her grandmother into her bedroom and waited while she removed one of the dresses from the peg on the wall. "I will wait for you in the living room." She patted Faith's arm and stepped from the room.

Faith slowly removed her wet clothes and smoothed the dress into place. How many years had it been since she dressed Amish?

In the living room her grandmother spotted her and clutched her hands together. "You always did look exactly like your *mamm*."

Faith settled into the rocker beside her. Quiet settled between them. Grandmother was waited for her to open up just like when Faith was a child. She wouldn't ask a single question. She'd wait. Like she had through all these years. Waiting for Faith to come home.

Good memories filled Faith's heart and brought a lump to her throat. She remembered sitting at her grandfather's feet while he read the Bible aloud to his family on Sundays, never imagining her idyllic child-hood would come to an end.

"I'm sorry. I should have realized what my father was doing. I should have tried to find out the truth sooner." Faith reached for her grandmother's hand again because holding it gave her a sense of peace.

"That is not your fault, child, and you are here now." Never a negative word. Not even for the man who had torn apart their family. This woman beside her was stronger than Faith would ever be.

Faith pulled in several cleansing breaths and struggled to control the tears that were so close. "Someone tried to kill me tonight." Saying the words aloud didn't make it any easier to accept. "No, not just someone. I know who tried to kill me. It was my brother-in-law. Blake's brother." She told her grandmother everything. "He killed Blake because he was going to turn himself in and implicate Vincent and the others." She shook her head. "And he killed his wife right in front of me. Cheryl was more than my sister-in-law—she was my friend. She came to the house because I called her. I showed her Blake's note. She couldn't believe what my husband had written." Her voice trailed off as the image of Cheryl's final seconds flashed through her mind.

While she and Cheryl tried to decide what to do with the evidence tucked in Faith's purse, Vincent forced his way into the house. He'd followed Cheryl there. When she'd confronted him with Blake's note, he'd grabbed Cheryl by the throat and pinned her against the wall. Cheryl begged her to take the note and leave, but Faith tried to get Vincent off her friend. He'd slugged her hard. And then he'd shot his wife. Panicked, Faith grabbed the note from where it had fallen, snatched her purse, and ran, barely making it to the car. She'd backed out of the garage when Vincent ran out shooting into the street behind her without caring about her neighbors. She'd floored the gas pedal and dodged the bullets flying all around her.

Faith sat up straighter at the thought of something she hadn't considered before. Vincent had told her the gun he used to kill Cheryl belonged to Faith, but how was that possible? Until Vincent barged into her home, he didn't know she even had any evidence. The last time she'd seen the weapon was when Blake locked it away in the safe he kept in his office. Her sleep-deprived brain hadn't considered Vincent might be lying until now. And if he'd lied about using her gun, then what else?

"Vincent can't afford to have the information on the thumb drive out there for someone to find. And there's always the chance if he lets me live—even if he does try to frame me for Cheryl's death—someone may believe my story. He can't let me live." She shivered at how close to killing her Vincent had come already. Minutes really, if Eli hadn't happened to come her way.

"He's a dangerous man, *Grossmammi*." The language of her childhood came back as easily as if drawing her next breath.

Disbelief replaced the tenderness on her grandmother's face. At one time, Faith couldn't imagine such an evil either.

"You must go to the sheriff, Granddaughter. He can help—"

Faith didn't let her finish. "That's not possible. Vincent is one of them. He'll know what to say to make them believe his story over mine. I can't go to the sheriff. At least not until I have the evidence back."

And to get it, she'd have to return to the creek as soon as possible. If she ever stood a chance at getting out from under Vincent's threat, there was no other choice.

Grandmother Sarah leaned closer. "What can I do to help?"

Despite her fear, Faith smiled. "Nothing. I'm sorry I brought my troubles to your door, but I didn't know where else to go. I've missed you so much. We've lost so much time."

Grandmother leaned in and hugged her tightly. "*Jah*, we have, but you must not hold on to the anger, Faith. It will tear you apart."

She'd told herself this many times. Forgiveness was as much a part of her healing as it was about letting go of her father's wrongdoings, yet no matter how hard she tried, she hadn't gotten there yet.

After Blake passed, her thoughts kept returning to her Amish life in West Kootenai. But could she stay? She'd traveled so far away from this Plain life. Gotten off track. More than anything, she wanted to change all that.

She jumped when a rap sounded from the front of the house. Grandmother Sarah patted her arm. "It's Eli." She rose and unlocked the door.

Eli stepped across the threshold. The frown on his face grabbed Faith's attention. Something had happened.

"I heard the vehicle again. It sounded close to the turnoff. It appears to be sitting still." His gaze homed in on Faith. "It could be the same truck that ran you off the bridge."

She was on her feet in an instant. "How did he find us so quickly?" Eli had stabled the horse and wagon. There would be nothing to lead Vincent to this house unless he somehow knew about her past.

Please, no.

Eli's dark eyes held hers. "If he is knowledgeable in tracking, he could quite possibly have seen the wagon tracks and followed."

The news threatened to break her. She rubbed a trembling hand across her eyes.

"Perhaps it isn't him," Eli said at her reaction. "There are many cars that travel the road by the creek. It could be someone passing through the community."

At this time of the night? Under these conditions? The likelihood of it being anyone other than Vincent was slim. She'd come all this way hoping her troubles would just disappear the moment she stepped foot on community property. Instead, she'd come close to dying. Involved her grandmother in her troubles. Had almost gotten Eli killed at the hands of a man who would stop at nothing to cover up his crimes.

"I will slip down to the road and take a look," Eli told them and headed out the door.

Faith couldn't let him go there alone while she hid in the house. "I'm coming with you."

Eli's forehead furrowed. "That's unwise. This man is dangerous, and he's looking for you. There's a chance he may not recognize me. You should stay with your grandmother."

"I'm coming," she insisted, expecting some more push back.

Something akin to admiration flashed in his brown eyes before he nodded. "As you wish."

He leaned inside and picked up the shotgun from where he'd placed it by the door. The need for the weapon reminded her again of the serious dangers Vincent presented.

It would be just the two of them against a man who was highly trained and motivated by having everything to lose.

Grandmother Sarah gathered her hand in hers. "Be careful. Both of you."

Faith forced a smile. "We'll be okay. Lock up behind us and don't open the door until we speak to you."

The fear in her grandmother's eyes hung heavily over Faith as the door closed. She hated the need to worry this precious woman, but the reality was Vincent had killed before. He wouldn't hesitate to take Grandmother's life if it benefited him.

Faith waited until the lock slid into place before she followed Eli from the porch and toward the woods that separated her grandmother's place from the road.

Newly fallen snow muted their footsteps. The only sound in the night was the noise the idling vehicle made close by. What if Vincent had left the truck running to draw them out? He could be hiding in the woods and waiting for them to come to him.

Shoving down the fear was hard but giving in to it made her vulnerable to mistakes. She couldn't afford a single false move if she wanted to live.

The man beside her remained silent as they walked.

Faith glanced around at the snowy wonderland and remembered how much as a child she'd loved roaming these woods. Exploring every inch with her *grossdaddi*.

Eli stopped so suddenly she was caught off guard. He barred the path in front of her. In an instant, those fond memories evaporated, and the reality of her situation pumped adrenaline through her veins.

"Do you see something?" she whispered.

"Jah." He pointed through the growth. "That's the same truck from earlier."

Her heart hiccupped. Vincent was right down the

road from her, and she knew what he was capable of. Just being this close to him scared the daylights out of her.

"What's he doing?" she asked. The truck had been sitting still for a while. The windows were foggy and she couldn't see inside it.

"Whatever it is, it can't be good." They exchanged a look. An uneasy feeling slipped between her shoulder blades. Was she risking their lives by being out here?

"Maybe we should go back. If he finds us here, he could try to finish what he started earlier."

The truck's interior light flashed. Vincent had opened the door, and he was getting out.

Eli grabbed her arm and tugged her behind the closest tree.

A tense breath slipped past her lips as footsteps headed into the woods in their direction. She tried to control her labored breathing. The last thing she wanted was to alert Vincent they were there.

Faith closed her eyes and prayed with all her heart as seconds ticked by. Finally, Vincent moved away, and she could breathe again. It sounded as if he was heading back to the truck. Why had he gotten out? Had he heard something and gone to investigate? She glanced back toward her grandmother's house. With the thick tree coverage, the house wasn't visible from the road.

A door was slammed shut.

"That was close," she whispered.

The truck pulled back onto the road. Its headlights flashed across the space where they hid as Vincent made a U-turn and started back toward the bridge.

Faith forced herself to leave the cover of the tree. The truck picked up speed as it headed down the road.

An object was tossed from the driver's-side window into the woods just past where they stood.

"Did you see that?" she asked Eli.

He nodded. "*Jah*, I did. I'm guessing he was looking for a place to get rid of something."

Vincent sped down the road. Soon, his taillights disappeared.

Faith hurried over to the spot where he'd tossed the item. As soon as she got close enough, she recognized it and the ground seemed to be taken out from underneath her. It was her purse. Vincent had found it. Did he have the thumb drive?

She bent over, picked up the purse and opened it.

"This is yours?" Eli asked, watching her.

"Yes." The only thing in the purse was a photo she'd saved of herself and Blake taken during happier times. She'd kept it because it reminded her of the man she'd fallen in love with. Not the person she hadn't known existed.

"It's not here." She held the empty purse in her hands. Her troubled gaze found Eli's.

"What's not in there?"

"The evidence that proves Vincent is a dirty cop and responsible for taking the life of his brother, my husband."

Eli's eyes widened. "This man is your brother-in-law? He killed your husband along with his wife?"

As hard as it was to admit her own ignorance, Eli deserved to hear the truth. Every ugly detail. "Yes. My last name is really St. Clair, but after everything that's happened, I don't want to be associated with that family." She stopped long enough to look at Eli. She couldn't imagine what he was thinking.

"Vincent and my husband were New York City detectives. He killed Blake because his brother was going to turn him in."

The shock on Eli's face was clear to see. "This is where you are living?"

She slowly nodded. "Yes. I moved to the city after I graduated from nursing school." Her fragmented thoughts returned to what occurred at the creek. She told him about what happened before he'd arrived. The frantic fall from the bridge. "Vincent started shooting as soon as I cleared the car. My purse popped open. I've no doubt my phone is gone. It's probably at the bottom of Silver Creek by now."

Faith gave a detailed account of what was on the thumb drive. "And there was a video. It showed Blake and Vincent discussing the upcoming murder of a rival dealer with a man I didn't recognize, but Blake made it a point to use his street name. Ghost." Even the name was frightening.

"Blake had obviously been compiling information to take down his brother, the rest of the dirty cops and Ghost for a long time. He left a note for me taped under his desk. He warned me not to go to any of the cops in the city for help." Faith gathered her jacket closer around her body and looked to Eli. "I don't know how widespread the corruption really is."

Terrified, she'd been convinced the conversation on the video was important, and so she'd sent a copy of it to her phone. Now, the information she'd need to bring down Vincent was missing. Without it she had nothing, and Vincent was determined to make her and the problem she represented disappear just as easily as he'd taken out Blake and Cheryl.

"I printed everything on the drive and placed it in my purse. The plastic bag containing the drive itself was hidden in my wallet." She shook her head.

"Even if there's the slightest chance Vincent doesn't have all the evidence, I have to go back to the creek. Finding those items may be my only chance to stop him from killing me."

Eli's frown deepened. "There's a good chance the documents were destroyed by the water. There could be nothing to save and this man will probably be expecting you to go back there. He'll be watching for you."

She of all people knew Vincent St. Clair's capabilities.

When she'd found the note from her husband almost a year to the day of his death, it had taken away part of her innocence. She'd always believed the police were the good guys. There to protect people. Yet Blake wrote that he and his brother had been on the take for years. Sometimes bad guys came disguised as men carrying badges.

"I know he will be." She'd need everything she could get to fight Vincent, including Eli's help. She couldn't do it on her own. Tonight had taught her that.

"He killed my husband, Eli. Vincent shot his brother and told me Blake died during a drug raid." She could still remember her reaction. The shock. The disbelief at hearing her husband was dead.

She'd been so naive. Had never imagined Vincent would be capable of doing such a despicable thing.

"My world collapsed," she said as they headed back to her grandmother's house. "I couldn't bring myself to go into Blake's office until a few weeks ago."

And then she'd learned everything she'd been told was a lie.

"I found the note by accident. Blake had taped a key there with it. The key fit a safe-deposit box in Upstate New York that contained the thumb drive."

"You had no idea your husband was involved in such crimes?" She heard the disbelief in his tone and couldn't blame him. If she were hearing this story for the first time, she'd probably have plenty of doubts too.

"I know how hard it is to imagine, but I had no idea." Blake had kept her insulated from his illegal dealings. "Looking back, those last few days before he'd died, something was troubling him." He'd barricaded himself in the office long into the night. He'd become jumpy and constantly checked the windows. Blake wouldn't tell her what was wrong, just that it was something with the job.

"I didn't know who to trust, only that I couldn't go to any of Blake's cop friends with the information."

"That must have been terrifying." The simple acceptance in Eli's tone drew her attention to him. An old memory from childhood came to mind. She was probably only six or seven. Her mother was supposed to be waiting to pick her up after school. Faith ran outside to find she wasn't there. She'd been scared, but Eli had walked her home and held her hand the entire time.

Up ahead, her grandmother's house appeared through the trees. The same sense of returning home filled her with longings of a simpler time. Yet nothing about her return here had been simple. Far from it.

"Vincent knows I have evidence against him because he read part of Blake's note. I have to get that drive back before he finds it."

Eli glanced up at the falling snow. The early spring storm continued to grow stronger and the weather was deteriorating quickly. "We'll never see it in this weather. At first light, we'll go back and search. If it's there, we'll find it."

With hours standing between her and being able to look for the drive, Faith's thoughts churned with worst-case scenarios. Undoubtedly, with or without the drive, Vincent would follow her to the ends of the earth to put her down.

Eli guided Sarah's buggy through the woods behind her place. Though he hated leaving Sarah alone, the kindly woman had assured him she would be *oke*. Eli confirmed both doors were locked, and Sarah had her husband's shotgun within arm's reach, just in case Vincent tied the homestead to Faith.

It was too risky to take the road back to Silver Creek, but he didn't want to go in on foot in case they ran into trouble. There was a good chance Vincent would be trolling the area around the creek looking for Faith. They'd need the buggy to escape.

The woman who had consumed his thoughts most of the night sat rigidly at his side. She wore her fear like a cloak tucked tight around her body. Faith hadn't said more than a handful of words since they'd left the house.

After his own sleepless night, Eli had risen well before dawn, unable to quiet his mind enough to rest. The things Faith told him rattled around in his mind. At each little sound outside he'd checked the window because he'd seen the lengths the man coming after Faith would go to keep his secrets.

"Eli?" Her soft voice interrupted his troubled thoughts, and he turned at the sound of his name. Faith's brows scrunched together as if she'd been trying to get his attention for a while.

"I'm sorry." He shook his head. "I'm a million miles away."

She smiled and his attention was drawn to the way it transformed her entire face. Those once-serious green eyes sparkled. Worry lines eased. The inquisitive little girl from his past had grown into a beautiful woman.

Beautiful?

He hadn't considered another woman beautiful before, and it felt as if he were betraying Miriam by the mere thought.

Heat crept up his neck, and his gaze shifted to the road ahead. Miriam held his heart still, but he and Faith had grown up together.

"When I first saw you, it took me only a second to remember how we knew each other," Faith was saying. "Your grandfather and mine were such good friends. You and I kind of fell into our friendship through them."

"*Jah*, they were *gut* friends, for sure. And you always hung out with your *grossdaddi*, as I recall." He cast a sideways look her way. "Whenever he visited my grandfather, you were at his side." He smiled at the memory. She'd been just a little thing back then. Much smaller than other kids in her class. It had brought out his protective instincts at an early age, especially when the bigger kids at school tried to pick on her.

"He was my hero," she murmured with a whimsical expression on her face. The look reminded Eli of the girl who used to follow him around. Always excited about every little thing.

"I remember Amos coming to the school to walk you home many times. He was a big man but kind to everyone. Unless they messed with his granddaughter." He winked at Faith. And whenever Amos or Faith's *mamm* were unable to see her home, Eli would take her to her grandparents.

"Yes, I was his little girl. He taught me so many things. We used to have these amazing adventures. He and my grandmother were my whole world back then. I thought *Grossdaddi* Amos hung the moon." She shook her head, and the smile disappeared as if something ugly had taken its place in her memory.

Like him, she had plenty of secrets. Some best left alone.

"It was a sad day when he passed," Eli said. Especially sad when Amos's wife was the only relative at the funeral. Though everyone in the community was there to support Sarah, she missed her family terribly. Her granddaughter in particular.

Years ago, Eli remembered overhearing conversations between his grandpa and Amos. They'd talk about Amos's son, Saul. How difficult the relationship had become between father and *sohn*. Saul seemed to resent the hard work associated with the Plain life. He wanted more than to be a farmer. Something Eli didn't understand at all. He couldn't imagine living anywhere other than among the Amish people.

The Silver Creek Bridge appeared in front of them. Eli's hands tightened on the reins as they drew closer, the events from the previous evening fresh on his mind. Even from their limited vantage point, the damaged guardrail was a stark reminder of what had happened the night before. How close Faith had come to dying. The danger that faced them now.

Today, there didn't appear to be any vehicles parked along the roadside. He wondered if Vincent had found the information Faith was counting on. As much as Eli wanted to be done with such an evil man, he had no doubt that someone who had gone to such lengths as to follow Faith all this way—and run her off the road—would not give up until she was dead.

Eli pulled back on the reins and brought the mare to a stop. Faith turned to him with a worried look on her face.

"Stay here. I'm going to check up at the road." He handed her the reins. "I'll be right back."

He hopped down and started through the snowy woods. As he walked, Eli checked the ground for any sign Vincent had been there. Only animal tracks disturbed the pristine countryside. Once he made sure the truck wasn't parked near the road, he returned to Faith.

"I think it's best if we leave the buggy here. Just in case," he added when her fear level rose before his eyes. "I didn't see any sign of him near the road, and there are no fresh tire tracks." Yet the hairs on the back of his neck assured him they were far from being out of danger.

Eli tied the reins to a sturdy tree branch and held out his hand to assist Faith as she used the buggy's step to reach the ground.

With her hand in his, another memory from childhood flew from its resting place in his mind. She'd been so young. Maybe even before she'd begun her schooling. Her grandfather had come to visit his friend at their family's newly operational lumber mill. Eli, several of his brothers and their *daed* had been there. The machines used to cut the trees into lumber were massive. Faith was curious. She'd snuck away when the grown-ups were talking and had gotten a little too close to the blade.

Eli had snatched her away before she could get hurt, but she'd been terrified. Tears falling down her cheeks, she'd clung to his hand as he brought her back to her grandfather. Their lives had been interlocked for many a year.

He glanced down and found her watching him. Those huge green eyes searching his face. Eli untangled his hand and pulled himself together.

After grabbing the shotgun from behind the seat, he headed down the slippery bank to the creek below. Faith followed at a slower pace, choosing her steps with care while he tried to understand what had gotten into him since seeing her again.

After Miriam's death, he'd gotten *gut* at shoving down his feelings. Maybe it was being back in West Kootenai. Seeing Faith again. She represented part of his childhood that was simpler.

At the edge of the water, a handful of papers were scattered around the bank. What appeared to be a couple of fast-food wrappers had floated ashore and caught on the brush.

Faith hurried past him and sifted through the ones on the ground with a hope that soon faded. "It's not them," she said with a defeated sigh. "The last time I saw my purse was in the water over there." She pointed to a spot midway under the bridge. "The thumb drive was in a small plastic ziplock bag. It has a blue closure." Faith glanced around the bank where more debris had floated from the car. "We should split up. I'll start over there."

They'd cover more ground if they went in different directions. Getting in and out of the area before Vincent returned was important. The last thing he wanted was to get caught out here in the open with a killer.

Eli headed along the bank. As he walked, he kept a careful eye on his surroundings. The road was just up from there. So far, there'd been nothing to indicate Vincent was close. Eli hoped it stayed that way.

A few more pieces of paper lay on the shore covered in mud. He picked up one. It was a flyer for a restaurant in New York. Eli kept walking.

As much as he wanted to believe Faith would find what she needed, the creek was fed by runoff from the year's heavy snowfall in the mountains. He couldn't remember the last time he'd seen the creek running so high. Chances were that anything as small as a plastic bag would have washed downstream by now. They might never find it.

The faintest of sounds grabbed his attention. Eli straightened and turned. He could no longer see Faith.

Sensing something was wrong, Eli started running back to where he'd left her when he heard her scream. He couldn't get back to her fast enough.

"Where is he? I know you didn't come here by yourself." Eli immediately recognized Vincent's voice. "Well, it doesn't matter. I'll take care of him after I've finished with you." Vincent's tone dripped with smugness and Eli ran harder. "I should have known Blake wouldn't go quietly. I cut him in on a way to make more than he ever could as a detective, and this is how he repaid me."

Eli stopped when he spotted Vincent looming over Faith and ducked behind a bush. He had to save her. If he could reach Vincent before the man spotted him…

"How could you kill your own brother?" Faith lunged for Vincent, but her moment of bravery was short-lived when he pointed a gun at her. She stopped short.

"The same way I killed Cheryl," he yelled. "She always was weak. In the past, she never would have dared question me until you got her involved. Killing her was easy. My brother used to be weak too, until he married you. Then he changed. Started questioning things he shouldn't have. I didn't have a choice. I had to kill him…just like I have to kill you." The fear on Faith's face was clear. Eli slowly eased from his hiding spot. "The person I work for won't take kindly to his livelihood being exposed. He wants you dead." With his finger on the trigger, Vincent prepared to follow through with his threat. Eli moved closer while trying to disguise the sound of his footsteps.

Faith's eyes widened when she spotted Eli. "If you kill me, the evidence I have against you and your boss will go public." She was trying to give Eli time to reach them. "Everyone will know what you've done."

The weapon in Vincent's hand lowered ever so slightly. "You're lying. I have the note Blake left you. The documents. I have everything." But just enough hesitation in his voice confirmed he wasn't sure.

When he was just a few feet from Vincent, Eli raised the shotgun. Vincent whirled at the tiniest of sounds.

"You! I told you to stay out of this."

Before Eli got off a single shot, Vincent fired his handgun. Eli hit the ground before the shot could take him out.

Vincent prepared to fire again. Eli leaped to his feet, grabbed the shotgun by the barrel, and swung. It connected with the side of Vincent's head before the man could get off another shot. The look of shock on Vincent's face was short lived. His eyes slammed shut and he dropped to the ground where he stood.

Eli's hands shook as he covered the space between himself and Faith. "Are you *oke*?" She managed a nod. "We have to go. Now. Before he wakes." Eli did a quick search of Vincent's pockets to make sure he didn't possess the evidence before he grabbed Faith's hand. Together, they started up the steep embankment, his boots slipping over the slick earth. The snow from the previous evening had turned to slush, and it was hard to gain traction.

Once they reached the buggy, Eli untied the reins, and they climbed up on the bench seat. He urged the mare back through the woods. It was too risky to take a direct path to Sarah's. They'd be leading Vincent straight to Eli's elderly neighbor. He'd have to find another way.

"I had no idea he was there until he was right on top of me." It was difficult for Eli to understand Faith's unsteady words. "He has Blake's letter and the printouts from the thumb drive."

"But he doesn't have the drive." Eli truly believed that. He glanced over his shoulder in time to see Vincent running toward them. He had the gun in his hand. In his rush to get them away from the man, Eli hadn't thought to grab Vincent's weapon.

"He's coming after us. Get down," Eli yelled. The words just cleared his lips when Vincent opened fire on them. The mare spooked and charged through the woods at a rapid pace.

Why hadn't he heard Vincent's truck before he ambushed Faith? The only answer was he'd parked it somewhere down the road and had been waiting for them to show up.

Once they were out of Vincent's line of sight, Eli headed the animal toward the shortcut he'd used as a kid. Behind them, an engine fired. Vincent was coming.

Faith held on to the bottom of the seat as Eli crossed the road onto a narrow path. "I hope you're right about the thumb drive. It could either be at the bottom of the creek or maybe it floated downstream. Either way, I have to go back."

After what happened just now, Eli didn't want her anywhere near the creek again. "It's too dangerous. I think it's time to go to the sheriff."

She barely let him finish. "I can't. Don't you understand? Vincent is willing to kill to cover up his crimes, and he's a cop." Her voice cracked with frustration and tears shone in her eyes. "He said he'd frame me for Cheryl's death. The police may be looking for me already. I can't go to the sheriff. Not without the drive."

Eli, of all people, understood how hard it was to clear your name, and he didn't want that for Faith.

"*Oke*, we won't go to the sheriff yet."

She held on to his gaze. "What if Vincent finds the drive first? It's all I have."

Eli reached for her hand. "It will be *oke*. You told him if anything happened to you the evidence would go public. Chances are, he'll think the drive is hidden somewhere else."

A relieved smile spread across her face, sweeping him back in time while he prayed his words proved to be true. For a moment, she was that little girl again, holding his hand as they walked home. That same smile on her face whenever he'd find a pretty rock along the way because he remembered she always picked them up in the schoolyard. She'd trusted him completely back then. He hoped she would now.

Eli's attention shifted from the pretty woman at his side to the overgrown path ahead. It had been years since he'd used it. Much had changed during that time.

The snow from last night's storm had probably melted on the road from the vehicles passing over it. Would Vincent see the tracks where the buggy crossed?

Eli listened. The truck continued down the road past the turnoff. A moment of relief was short-lived when a far more disturbing thought occurred. Vincent had once been part of Faith's family. What had she told him about her past?

The thought of Vincent showing up at Eli's innocent neighbor's house terrified him.

"Does this man know you were once Amish?" Eli frowned and watched her reaction.

Faith pinched the bridge of her nose. "I don't know. Both my husband and sister-in-law knew about my past. It's possible they might have mentioned it to Vincent."

They rode in silence for the time being while Eli thought about what she'd said. The ways of the *Englisch* world were beyond his understanding, and he was glad of it.

The community shops appeared in front of them. Eli eased the buggy toward the back and into the woods there.

"Best not to take any chances," he said when Faith looked his way. "He could be anywhere around the community. I wouldn't put it past him to try to get information from the shop owners." Sarah was at the foremost in his thoughts. Was she safe? The sooner they reached her house the better he'd feel.

"How long have you lived near my grandmother?" Faith asked as if she were searching for something to take her mind off what was happening. The question surprised him. A look her way indicated she was watching him. He knew so little about her life beyond what she'd told him. Sarah hadn't mentioned her granddaughter. Did Faith know about his ugly past?

Don't go back there...

He forced himself to answer. "About a month. I lived in Libby before I moved back to West Kootenai, and now I live in your former home."

"I didn't realize you'd left the community," she said in a halting voice. "I remember your family well. You had lots of brothers, but Mason was the one you were closest to, right? You two were always together."

He flinched as if she'd struck him. She had no idea the pain her words brought forth. Not a second went by that he didn't remember the things he'd lost because of love. The guilt he carried. Because of him, his brother had walked away from their faith. If it hadn't been for him, Mason would still be Amish. If it hadn't been for him, Miriam would still be alive. And if he failed Faith now, she might end up dead just like Miriam.

THREE

Growing up, she'd been a child of the light. Terrified of the darkness because it held so many secrets. Bad things she couldn't see.

Her *mamm* had always been there to comfort her. She'd done her best to make sure her daughter knew there was nothing to be afraid of, yet Faith had struggled with the fear long into adulthood, and she had no idea why.

She stared out the kitchen window as dark clouds hung low around the farm, turning the midday to twilight. Despite that she'd seen no sign of Vincent since she and Eli left the creek, letting herself relax was impossible.

Every little sound sent her jumping. Vincent was still out there somewhere. Twice he'd seen her with Eli. He must know she was hiding somewhere in the Amish community.

"What do you see out there, child?" Faith jerked at the sound of her grandmother's voice. They'd been clearing away the dishes after the midday meal, yet throughout the simple chore, Faith's attention had remained on the darkness outside.

"Nothing. I'm just…" She didn't finish. Wasn't sure what she was about to say. Instead, she squeezed her grandmother's arm and carried the plates she held in her hands to the sink.

Grandmother Sarah took them from her. "Eli will help figure this out. You can trust him. He's a *gut* man."

Faith could see how much her grandmother adored Eli, but he couldn't stop a monster from stalking her. Could anyone?

"You two have really gotten close, haven't you?" She tried not to let the dark thoughts take over. She was safe here. Vincent didn't know where she was.

Grandmother Sarah's face brightened. "*Jah*, we have. He reminds me a lot of your *daed* before…" She didn't have to finish. Faith understood. Her mother tried to protect Faith from her father's dark moods as a child. And then that summer had happened. The argument between her father and *Grossdaddi* had been terrifying for a little girl to witness. The next thing Faith knew, she and her mother were being forced to leave the only way of life they'd ever known.

After she left home and moved to New York, her parents had died in a car accident. The police who investigated the accident believed excessive speed was the cause. Had her father's anger been out of control, costing both him and his wife their lives?

Eli stepped into the kitchen, capturing Faith's attention. He wore his hat and coat. "I'm going to feed the animals in the barn," he told her grandmother and then shifted his gaze to Faith. "Will you come with me? I could use an extra hand with the chores." Though he smiled, she knew the real reason. Eli didn't want her to be out of his sight for a minute.

Grandmother Sarah squeezed her close. "Go with him, *boppli*. I have some quilting to work on. I promised Eva Klimer I'd finish the quilt before her daughter gives birth soon."

Still, Faith hated leaving her grandmother with Vincent lurking around the community. Hurting her grandmother would mean nothing to him.

"You could come with us?" Faith asked.

Her grandmother shook her head. "I will be fine, and I have work to do."

The barn wasn't that far from the house, and they wouldn't be gone for long. "Alright but come lock the door behind us." Faith double-checked the back door to make sure it was still locked.

"*Jah*, I will." Grandmother Sarah held her hand as they walked to the door together. She took down her warmest cloak from the peg by the door and wrapped it around Faith's shoulders. "Use this one. It's getting colder."

The familiar scent of her grandmother clung to the garment. Faith drew in a deep breath, found comfort in the familiar and stepped outside with Eli.

Grandmother Sarah's smile was the last thing she saw before the door closed. The lock slid into place. And the nightmare she faced hit her head-on.

"There's been no sign of him," Eli assured her as if he'd sensed the necessity.

She nodded and stepped from the porch beside him. They walked toward her grandparents' old barn.

Eli removed the board holding the doors together and opened them. So many good memories waited for her inside these four walls. It was here that she'd learned how to ride. Helped her *grossdaddi* milk the cow.

Faith waited just inside the door while Eli struck a match to the lantern and the barn was illuminated. The light caused some of her fears to flee.

The cow was stabled here along with her grandmother's old mare.

"How's she really doing?" She swung toward Eli and asked.

He'd taken the milking stool down in preparation. His expression softened. "Most days she is *gut*. The cold is hard, though. She tells me her arthritis gets worse every year. I can tell she's happy you're back."

What he said broke her heart. "I didn't know. My father told me my grandparents were dead." She shook her head with regret. "I shouldn't have believed him. He was so angry with *grossdaddi*."

Eli's jaw tightened. "That's a horrible thing to do to a *kinna*."

"It was. I will never understand why my father did the things he did," she said with a sigh. "Or why he hated this way of life so much."

Eli didn't understand either. "When did you realize your *grossmammi* was still alive?"

"Not too long ago. I contacted my grandmother's friend, Mrs. Stoltzfus at the bakery, and found out the truth."

"I'm sorry," he said. The sympathy in his eyes almost brought her to tears. "But you are here now and your *grossmammi* is happy to have you home."

Faith turned away. Was she home? Did she dare let herself return to the place she longed for the most? She'd already brought something dreadful to this peaceful community. How many more innocent people would have to suffer because Vincent had followed her to West Kootenai?

She pulled in an unsteady breath and let that worry go for the moment. *Don't take on tomorrow's troubles before their time*, her grandmother used to say.

Though it had been years since Faith had performed farm chores, she scooped a bucket of oats and carried them to the mare her grandmother spoke about in her letters.

"How are you today, Jenny?" The mare knickered her thanks, and Faith stroked her muzzle before bringing over some water that Eli had pumped from the well earlier.

Once she'd finished, Faith continued to pet the mare while watching Eli as he milked. He'd tipped his hat back on his strong forehead, his full attention on the task at hand, and he was unaware of her.

As a little girl of ten, she'd thought Eli was the most handsome man alive, except for her grandfather. And he still was. Eli was a good man who had gone out of his way to help her when she had no one else to turn to. Spending time with him again made her wonder what her life would have been like if she'd stayed. Perhaps she and Eli would have married.

At one time, she'd thought herself blessed beyond everything to have found someone like her husband. But if Blake had been able to fool her so easily, how could she ever trust another man with her heart?

Eli looked up and found her watching him. She turned away, paid extra attention to the mare and tried to calm her chaotic pulse.

Once the milking was finished, Eli carried the pail to the door.

With a final pat for Jenny, Faith stepped out into the chilly afternoon.

"I fed the chickens and gathered the eggs earlier," Eli told her. "If you're ready, we can go back to the house."

He shut the barn back up and lifted the pail. He started for the house with Faith beside him. They'd covered only a few feet when something captured her attention and she froze. The noise of an engine disturbed the peace and quiet of the countryside. The vehicle wasn't just passing by on the nearby road. It had turned onto the path leading past her grandmother's house. It was coming their way. Even before she had a visual of the vehicle, she knew. Vincent was here.

Eli dropped the bucket of milk and grabbed Faith's arm. "We've got to get out of sight before he reaches the road out front." He tugged her along beside him to the shelter of some trees while all sorts of dreadful thoughts flew through his mind. If this was Vincent, none of them was safe here any longer.

His heart drummed a frantic rhythm as the vehicle crept along the road. No one drove that slowly deliberately.

From his hiding spot, Eli could tell the truck was Vincent's. Did he know this was Faith's grandmother's property, or was he checking all the roads around in the community for them?

The truck eased past Sarah's home and continued until it was even with the place where he and Faith were hiding.

"He's stopping," Faith murmured, her tone heavy with fear.

Eli inched away from the tree in time to see the truck stop. He couldn't tell what Vincent was doing inside, but the man was armed and extremely dangerous, and they were out in the open and vulnerable.

Seconds ticked by while Eli kept his attention on the truck. Suddenly, the driver's door opened, and Vincent jumped out. Eli ducked back behind the tree when Vincent started through the woods and onto Sarah's property. Eli guessed for someone who had killed, trespassing meant nothing.

Faith inched nearer. Alarm in her eyes. Eli slipped his arm around her waist and tugged her close.

The noise of Vincent moving through the underbrush warred with Eli's panicked breathing.

Please, Gott, help us.

Footsteps halted near their hiding spot. Labored breaths appeared to come from just a few feet away.

Vincent entered Eli's line of sight. It was only a matter of time before they were spotted.

Eli handed Faith the shotgun and pushed her out of sight. The noise grabbed Vincent's attention. Before Eli had time to pull in a breath, Vincent had his gun drawn and pointed at him.

With his pulse skyrocketing, Eli tried not to show fear though plenty ran through his body.

"This is private property, and you are not welcome here. I want you to leave. Now." He moved closer to Vincent and away from Faith.

The man didn't react to the request. He kept the weapon on Eli. "I know you. You're the one who was with her before." Vincent looked him up and down. "Where is she?"

Eli stood his ground. "She left and you have no right to be here. You're trespassing."

Vincent didn't budge. "I know she didn't leave because she has no means to. She's somewhere in this community, and you know where." The words seethed from Vincent's lips as he stepped closer. "Is this your house? I've been going house to house, but no one seems to know anything about Faith being here. I'm guessing that's because you've been hiding her." He moved toward where Faith hid.

Eli blocked his path. "There's no one here other than me and my elderly neighbor."

Vincent eyed him suspiciously. "I don't believe you. You're protecting her. She's in the house."

"I told you there's no one inside the house except for my neighbor. It's time for you to go."

Vincent lowered his gun a fraction and released an angry breath. "Look, I know you people are peaceful and don't like violence, so if you want to keep it that way, stay out of this. I'll get her and leave." He paused with a nasty look on his face. "I'd hate for something bad to happen to you because you stuck your nose where it didn't belong."

Before Eli could respond, the tiniest of sounds came from close by.

Vincent swung that direction. "What was that?" His gaze drilled into Eli, who fought to keep a blank expression.

"I don't know what you're talking about. I didn't hear anything."

Vincent started toward the tree. Eli couldn't let him get to Faith. Acting on instinct alone, he dove for the man and tackled Vincent before he reached the tree.

"Run!" Eli yelled and wrestled for control of Vincent's weapon. The man slugged him hard, sending Eli's head snapping sideways.

"Stop right there." Faith stepped from behind the tree with the shotgun pointed.

Vincent swung toward her. Momentarily distracted, Eli grabbed for his weapon and managed to pry it free from Vincent's hand.

Eli scrambled to his feet and hurried over to Faith while keeping the handgun trained on Vincent.

"On your feet," he ordered.

The man rose and raised his hands. "Alright. There's no need to get testy. I'll leave." Vincent tossed Faith a nasty look. "But this isn't over. I'll be back for you." With that parting threat, he turned on his heel and started walking to the truck.

Eli didn't lower the weapon until Vincent reached the vehicle. With a final angry glance, Vincent climbed into the truck and eased it around.

All Eli could think about was that the man who had tried to kill both of them now knew where they were staying. He didn't trust Vincent one little bit. He'd park the truck out of sight and wait. Give them a false sense of security. They had to escape before Vincent returned to finish the job. When he did, he'd take them all out, because he couldn't afford to leave any witnesses behind to tell of his deadly acts.

FOUR

"I can't believe that just happened." Faith's hands were shaking. She couldn't believe Vincent had been just a few feet away.

"He'll come back. We can't stay here," Eli told her.

She had no doubt. She'd been so certain Vincent would kill Eli.

Eli tucked the handgun into his jacket pocket and took the shotgun from her. "We can go to my home. It's hidden from the path that runs in front of Sarah's place. If you aren't looking for it, you wouldn't know a house was there."

His home had once been hers. So many good memories were made there. And just as many bad ones.

Together they started for the house at a fast pace. Faith climbed onto the porch steps and called out to her grandmother. "It's us. Open the door." Even with Eli close, she felt exposed. Her eyes grazed the gloomy afternoon. The truck's engine sounded close.

"I can't tell if he's sitting still or moving," Eli said.

Faith looked up at the persistent storm clouds that had turned the day cold. Though there was no sign of

Vincent or the truck in her limited line of sight, she couldn't help but believe time was running out.

Eli leaned past her and knocked again while her thoughts chased over themselves.

Her grandmother's slow footsteps headed toward them. Locks slid open. Grandmother Sarah opened the door, her worried gaze jerking between them. *"Was iss letz?"* She stepped aside to let them pass. As soon as Eli crossed the threshold, he closed the door and locked it.

"He's been here." The words rushed out and Faith grabbed a breath before continuing. "The man who forced me off the bridge was here on your property just now. He threatened to search the house. If Eli hadn't stopped him, he would have. We must leave, Grandmother. It's not safe for us to stay here under the circumstances."

Her grandmother's eyes grew large as she struggled to comprehend what her Faith told her. "But this is my home." She didn't understand there was no longer an option.

Faith clasped her hands and her grandmother focused on her. "If we stay, he will come back. He could kill all of us."

Grandmother Sarah flinched at those disturbing words. A gentle woman who had never met a bad man could not understand the depth of evil in Vincent's heart.

Eli hurried over to the window and looked out. "I don't see him yet." He turned from the window. "Quickly, Sarah. Pack some of your things. You and Faith will stay at my house until it is safe to come back."

Grandmother Sarah shook her head. "But Eli, my *mann* built this home before we wed. How can I leave it?"

Faith understood the reasons why her grandmother didn't wish to go. She couldn't imagine how difficult it would be to leave the one place you'd called home since you were but a young woman.

"It won't be forever. Just until we know it's safe to return. Come with me and I'll help you gather your things." Faith clutched her hand and tugged her toward the bedroom she'd shared with her husband.

Grandmother Sarah moved as if she were in a trance. "I can't believe this is happening. Why is this man doing such things?"

Explaining Vincent's actions was impossible. "He's a bad man without a conscience."

Faith pulled the weathered suitcase that had been in the family since Grandmother Sarah was young out from under the bed. Placing it on the bed, she walked to the pegs where Sarah's dresses hung, gathered them and placed the dresses inside.

Grandmother Sarah rose and placed her arm around Faith's waist. The strength in her touch surprising. "I am so sorry you have to go through this, my *boppli*, but with Eli's help, we will all be safe again."

If only it were that simple. But without the drive, she had no proof of Vincent's crimes. And while she believed he was not telling the truth about manipulating the evidence to make her appear guilty of killing his wife, he was quite capable of swaying his fellow law enforcement agents into believing his story. Vincent was setting the trap. He'd make the claim he had no choice but to kill her.

"We should hurry. He's probably watching the house now. We can slip out the back."

Grandmother Sarah nodded. "I am ready. Let's get Eli."

Faith grabbed the suitcase, and she and her grandmother returned to the living room where Eli still stood near the window keeping careful watch. He turned as they approached.

"Is there any sign of him?" Faith set down the suitcase and stepped to the window. The storm that had threatened most of the day was releasing snow and ice on the countryside.

"*Nay*, but we should get out of here while we still can."

As Eli lifted the suitcase and started toward the back of the house, a truck eased onto her grandmother's drive.

"Oh, no."

Eli jerked toward her, his brow deep with furrows. "What's wrong?" He hurried back to her side.

She pointed out the window. "He's here." Vincent's truck headed straight for the house.

"Hurry." Eli gathered Grandmother Sarah close and headed to the back door. "Be as quiet as you can," he told them. "Head for the woods bordering our two properties."

Faith slipped out the back door with her grandmother. Eli clicked the lock on the doorknob, closed the door and followed them.

At the front of the house, the truck stopped. Seconds passed and a vehicle door slammed shut. Faith's worried gaze flew to Eli's. There wouldn't be time to reach the woods.

"The equipment building off to the right. It's been years since it's been used. We can go in through the side door. The building is in bad shape. Maybe he won't look at it too closely," Eli whispered.

The building he spoke of had been one big playground for Faith as a child. She'd climb on the tractor and pretend to drive it. When she got a little older, her grandfather let her steer while he worked. It was a defining moment for a little girl.

With her grandmother's hand tucked in hers, they crossed the yard to the building where *Grossdaddi*'s old farming equipment was still stored.

A noise came from the front of the house. It sounded as if the front door had been forced open. Had Vincent broken into the house? Faith shouldn't have been surprised Vincent hadn't thought twice about breaking into the home. The man had killed two people that she knew of.

Once Vincent reached the back of the house, he'd be able to see them through the windows. They had to get out of sight quickly.

She and Eli pushed and shoved to budge the door. It squeaked in protest as it opened, and Faith was terrified Vincent would hear.

Eli closed the door after them. An unnerving silence permeated the building. Were they sitting ducks? The only working entrance into the building was the door they'd forced open. The large double-doors that grandfather used to drive the tractor through had fallen in on themselves long ago. Someone had attempted to patch them but had given up and boarded them. There would be no escaping that way.

The tractor sat rusting to the ground. Several farm

implements were in worse shape. The Amish helped those in need around the community. She had no doubt Eli would do everything he could for Grandmother, but Eli hadn't been home for long. How had her grandmother gotten by before?

A tingle of apprehension shot between Faith's shoulders. She was trapped inside a nightmare that kept getting worse.

Faith scrambled over to where Eli stood. This side of the building faced the back of the house.

"I can't see what's going on inside the house." Eli peered through some of the gaping boards in the wall. She did the same. Nothing moved near the back windows. What was Vincent doing in there?

The state of the decaying building broke her heart. Several boards were loose. Snow had piled up inside. Multiple gaping holes in the roof above where the tractor sat covered in snow left the machine open to the elements.

"I see him." Eli's whispered words brought her attention back to the house in time to see the back door fly open and slam against the wall, bouncing off it several times. The rage on Vincent's face sent Faith scrambling backward. She'd seen that look before. When he'd killed his wife. Tried to shoot her at the creek. It served as a deadly reminder of Vincent St. Clair was capable of.

He huffed out several breaths that fogged the misty air in front of him. Vincent reminded her of a rampaging bull as he stormed down the steps and looked around the property with a wild expression on his face.

For one brief second, he stared straight at the building where they hid. Faith clasped her hand over her mouth to keep from making a sound.

Vincent's attention shifted to the chicken coop. He stomped across the yard with a purposeful gate and threw open the door. Chickens squawked as he entered their domain. Several flew from the coop and landed across the yard like a small invasion.

"My chickens," Grandmother Sarah whispered. She'd told Faith all about her laying hens in her letters. She spoke of each bird as a friend.

Faith hugged her grandmother close and watched Vincent swat at chickens as he stormed from the coop huffing and puffing his anger.

The barn was the next one in his path of rage.

It was only a matter of time before he came here. "Do you think we have time to get to the woods once he enters the barn?" Faith asked Eli while keeping her focus on the man moving toward them one building at a time. It was like watching a horror show. Vincent entered the barn with complete disregard for the animals inside.

Before Eli answered, Vincent appeared in the open door again. His fury grew with each failure. He left the barn doors wide open.

"The animals." Grandmother Sarah's tender heart was focused on the creatures in the barn.

"It will be okay." But Faith wasn't sure she believed it. Vincent had everything to lose, and she stood between him and freedom. He'd do whatever was necessary to end her existence and anyone else's who got in his way.

"He disappeared around behind the barn," Eli said with a doubtful tone.

She had a feeling she knew. "He's checking the woods to see if we went that way."

"It won't take him long before he comes this way." Eli glanced around the inside. On the opposite wall, several boards had worked their way loose and were barely hanging by a few nails. Eli pointed to them. "Over there."

They headed for the boards when the sound of footsteps tromping their way froze Faith in her tracks. She claimed Eli's gaze. "He's coming."

The truth had just cleared her lips when Vincent confirmed their worst fears. "I know you're in there. Did you really think you could hide from me?" He laughed. Chills ran up her arms. "You should have stayed in New York. Kept your mouth shut. Now I have to take care of you." Vincent's frightening voice appeared right outside the door they'd entered. "You and those innocent people with you will have to die."

Grandmother Sarah clutched Faith's arm when the sound of something being moved replaced the silence.

Peering through the boards, Faith was horrified at what happened. Vincent muscled one of the old farming implements from the side of the building to the front of the door. He wanted to make sure they weren't able to escape that way. What did he have planned? The question still chased through her head when Vincent headed to the back porch and grabbed something.

"Oh, no," Eli said. He pointed to the can in Vincent's hand. "That's gas. He's going to burn the building down with us in it."

The depth of wickedness in this man's heart was beyond Eli's comprehension. He couldn't move as the scene unfolded before his eyes with deadly intent. Vincent tossed gas around the outside wall where he stood. Eli had glimpsed the barrel of a handgun holstered under his jacket.

"Where did he get that second gun?" Eli whispered in amazement. He couldn't believe Vincent had found another weapon.

"He's a cop," Faith reminded him. "He probably has several backups in the truck."

Powerless to do anything, Eli watched Vincent strike the match. The structure would go up like a tinderbox of dried Montana wood. They'd have only a matter of minutes to get out with their lives.

Eli pulled Faith and Sarah close as Vincent's silhouette moved around the building, visible through the gaping holes.

Whoosh! The sound left nothing to his imagination. The fire took life, crawling up the exterior wall on the opposite side from the loose boards. If they didn't act quickly, their exit path would soon be engulfed.

The acrid scent of smoke poured into the building.

Eli squinted through the fog and located where Vincent stood watching with a satisfied smile on his face.

"We have to go now." Eli grabbed Sarah's hand and tried not to think about the images of his sweet Miriam desperately searching for a way out of the blazing inferno.

Sarah clutched his jacket, and he wished he could spare her this anxiety, but he wasn't about to let her or anyone else die here in this building because of a bad man.

They reached the wall where the boards were the loosest. "He's still up front. With all the noise of the fire and the smoke, we should be able to get out without him seeing us. Run for the cover of the woods. Sarah, take off your cloak and wrap over your head and shoulders for protection. Don't think about what you're doing. Just go."

Sarah's frightened eyes clung to his. "It will be *oke*," he assured her. "Go, Sarah."

Hunched over, Sarah slipped through the opening and ran. Eli watched until she was safely in the woods. But the fire was intensifying. He turned to Faith. "Go. Quickly. I'll be right behind you." The flames were spreading rapidly across the decaying roof.

Faith hesitated only a second before following her grandmother's path through the opening. The blaze continued to burn red hot as it slithered down the wall toward the missing boards and the only means of escape. Once she cleared the building, Faith ran after her grandmother.

It was his turn now. Eli glanced over his shoulder. It wouldn't be long before the walls collapsed. The roof had already begun to cave in on itself.

Eli tucked the shotgun inside his jacket and started through the hole in the wall. Flames singed the hair on his hands. The heat was intense, and he held a deadly weapon in his hand. If the flames reached the shotgun shells and handgun in his pocket or in the gun tucked under his jacket, it could have deadly results.

Though it took only a couple of seconds to get through the space, with flames licking all around him, it felt like an eternity. His jacket caught fire in several places. Eli slapped at the flames with his hat while thankful that the noise of the fire's roar helped drown the sound of his movements.

He clamped the hat back on his head and headed toward the spot where he'd seen Faith and Sarah disappear. By now, the blaze made it hard to see anything. His eyes streamed from the smoke.

The roaring fire became like a living beast calling for vengeance. Gobbling up everything in its path. A chilling sight and one that had roots in Eli's past.

He'd only seen the aftermath of the fire in Libby that took his *fraa*'s life. Now he'd experienced firsthand the horror involved, and it was a struggle to hold it together when he thought about what Miriam had gone through. It somewhat comforted him to know that Miriam had died from smoke inhalation long before the fire claimed the house.

Eli shoved aside those heartbreaking memories and ran for the woods. He kept a careful watch over his shoulder, expecting Vincent to materialize behind him.

Once Eli reached the trees, he pulled in several needed breaths and coughed the toxic smoke from his lungs.

"You're still on fire," Faith exclaimed and beat out the flames with her uninjured hand.

Eli took off the jacket and threw it on the ground. Once he'd finished stamping out the fire, he clasped Faith's wrist, humbled by her willingness to disregard her own well-being for him.

"Let me have a look." He examined the burns carefully. "They are not too serious." He scooped up a handful of snow and placed it over the burns on her hand. "I have something at my house that will help with the pain."

He'd gotten used to taking care of himself during the past two years. Living a simple life. Choosing not to draw attention. Far different from when he was younger. He'd been ambitious. Desired to do better for his wife and child. He'd wanted to be the man she'd believed him to be. When she'd died, the future—his ambitions—had turned to so many ashes.

Coming on the heels of losing Miriam, it just about destroyed him when the police had told him they had evidence the fire was set deliberately and believed he had done it. They'd searched his property countless times. Had taken him into the station. Questioned him for hours. Insisted he knew more about the fire than what he'd told them.

At the time, the pain he felt at losing his *fraa* was so intense that he didn't much care what happened physically to him. He couldn't imagine life without Miriam. The days stretched to months. Living in the barn on his property and working as many hours as he could just to shut out the horror of losing his wife and child.

Eli swallowed deeply and realized he still held Faith's wrist in his hands. The confused look on her face assured him she'd been trying to get his attention.

He let her go and faced the terrifying scene behind them. The building was now completely engulfed and had begun to crumble.

Where was Vincent?

"We should keep moving," he said in a low voice. "This man is capable of anything. With all the smoke and flames, we'd never see him in time."

Keeping Faith and Sarah close, he headed through the dense woods at a fast pace. He prayed they would be safe at his home. Though it was some distance from Sarah's place, was it enough?

With the fire burning so intensely, not much would

be left inside the structure except smoldering ashes. Would they be enough to satisfy Vincent, or would he search the entire surrounding landscape?

The snowfall hadn't stuck to the ground where the heavily populated trees kept everything including sunlight out. Heat from the fire would melt any accumulation around the outside of the building and vanish any evidence of them getting away.

Through all of his chaotic thoughts, a sound penetrated. An engine.

Eli stopped walking. "Do you hear that? He's leaving." He cocked his head and listened. The truck eased from the property. He couldn't believe it. Vincent had gone to all the trouble of setting the fire to kill them, but he wouldn't wait to be sure they were dead.

Faith stood close by his side, watching the smoke plume up through the trees. "Maybe he's afraid someone from the community will spot the fire and come to put it out."

It made sense. The Amish watched out for each other. But whether or not Vincent knew this didn't matter. Something had spooked him enough to make him fall backward. Eli believed he wouldn't go far. He'd wait for the fire to burn itself out then return to ensure they were dead.

If the wind shifted, the fire might spread to Sarah's home. Eli couldn't allow that to happen.

"I still can't believe he is willing to burn us alive to save himself," Faith said in shocked disbelief. "He has to be stopped."

Eli agreed with her, but the only way would be to find the evidence Faith's husband gathered. Which meant, one way or another, they had to go back to the creek.

"I have to stop the fire from spreading. Why don't you take your grandmother and go to my house?"

Faith searched his face before shaking her head. "It's too much for one person. Let me help you." She turned to her grandmother. "Can you make it to Eli's house alone?"

Sarah's troubled expression didn't ease any, but she nodded. "*Jah*. I can make it."

"Good. Go ahead of us and stay inside. I'll bring your suitcase later." When Sarah hesitated, Faith assured her they would be okay. "Hurry, Grandmother."

With her cloak clutched tightly around her body, Sarah turned and picked her way through the foliage toward Eli's home.

Were he and Faith walking into a trap by trying to put out the fire? Vincent could have parked the truck off somewhere and walked back.

He prayed under his breath for their safety and kept close to Faith in case trouble came.

Eli removed his singed jacket and placed it over Faith's shoulders as they reached the clearing. He couldn't explain it, but that same protective instinct he'd experienced when he and Faith were younger had resurfaced.

"Thank you," she murmured as if the gesture meant the world to her.

He'd protect her with everything he had. No matter what, he wasn't going to let Vincent hurt her again.

With Faith by his side, he stepped into the clearing while the hackles on the back of his neck alerted him to the importance of working quickly. Smoke covered the farm. Even if Vincent were right on top of them, it would be impossible to see him with all the smoke.

The wind shifted the plume away for them. Eli scanned the area near the road. "I don't see his truck." He turned to Faith. "Do you?"

She shook her head. "I don't, but I feel he's close. If that were me, I wouldn't leave."

"I'll draw some water from the well and start fighting the fire. Sarah keeps extra buckets near the back door."

While Faith retrieved the buckets, Eli headed to the well on the other side of the barn where he kept a bucket for drawing the daily water.

At this point, there would be no saving the building, and there was no phone nearby to call the fire department. It would be up to them to prevent the fire from spreading to the house. The barn and chicken coop were some distance away, and the wind had shifted off from being a threat to them.

On his way, Eli herded the chickens into the coop and shut the door.

After he'd secured the barn doors, he lowered the bucket with a splash. He quickly hauled it up and started for the blaze.

Faith met him halfway with four extra buckets.

"Carry only what you can and leave the rest," he told her. The fire burned so hot that it was hard to get close enough, but he did his best and soaked the ground near to the house.

Working together, he and Faith carried buckets of water to the smoldering site.

When Eli dumped the last one onto the soaked remains, he surveyed the scene. "The fire appears to be contained. Let's get out of here before he returns."

As he glanced at the destroyed building, he was grateful the fire hadn't spread. Though the tractor and several farming implements were ruined, the cost could have been far worse with their lives. He'd help Sarah clean up the mess once this man was no longer a threat.

Once they reached the place where they'd left Sarah's suitcase, Eli picked it up. He went over everything in his head and still couldn't believe the man's ruthlessness. He voiced his thoughts aloud.

"He stands to lose his freedom if not his life," Faith said with a sigh. "I have no doubt the man he and Blake worked for will be furious when he realizes his drug empire is being threatened." Nothing she said eased Eli's worries. "Vincent's probably waiting until dark to come back. He'll search every square inch of the place looking for proof that we're dead."

"After getting a taste of what Vincent is like, I can't imagine the level of violence the man he works for is capable of." Eli found it hard to believe someone in law enforcement would allow their convictions to be compromised in such a way. All for money.

She and Eli continued to move through the overgrowth.

"Blake told me about such men, but I had no idea he worked for one." She shook her head. "These men pump drugs into the city at an alarming rate, and they take out any competition standing in their way."

Faith kept her attention ahead of them. "At the time, I didn't have any idea what Blake was up to, but now—looking back through different eyes—there were signs. I guess at the time I didn't want to see them."

Being a trusting person had its downside. Eli couldn't imagine the betrayal she'd experienced by someone she loved.

"I should have seen the truth." She lifted her shoulders. "All the expensive gadgets Blake would come home with. The gifts he bought me. All of it was far more than we could afford on our salaries. Blake told me he'd worked overtime to pay for everything, but he never really did. In the beginning, I worked the night shift at the hospital, so I had no way of knowing when he got home at night." She grew quiet for a time.

"When did you realize he wasn't working overtime?" Eli found himself curious about her marriage to this man. She'd loved him dearly.

"A few years after we bought the house, I started working regular hours. Blake was always home before me. Usually doing something in his office. I walked in on him one time, and he appeared nervous. When I came into the room, he shut the desk drawer as if he didn't want me to see what was inside." She shook her head. "But I was so naive. I trusted Blake. Once he passed away, I found out he'd paid the house off within the first year."

Eli shot her a look. "From dirty money?"

She nodded. "Yes. After I read his note, I knew I had to get out of that house. I was literally living in a crime scene." She glanced over her shoulder. "What Vincent did back there is nothing compared to what the man he works for will do to him if he doesn't take care of the threat I pose."

Eli struggled to understand how such men existed. "We should be safe enough at my place. The house itself is hidden from view of the road by the mountain.

If you didn't know it was there you would miss it." He stopped when he realized he wasn't telling her anything she didn't know. His house had once been her home.

Most people outside the community didn't realize another house past Sarah's property existed. The road leading to it was little more than a path. Eli had enough room to get his wagon in and out, but he was grateful for the seclusion.

He hoped Vincent wouldn't think to look that closely at the mountain because if he came that way, they'd be blocked by a sheer wall of stone.

He'd known Vincent was dangerous after the bridge incident, but the seriousness of the situation had been driven home to him with deadly accuracy upon their fiery attack at Sarah's.

With that much rage inside Vincent, how could Eli and Sarah stop him? Somehow, Eli had to find a way to convince Faith to speak with the sheriff. Though he understood her concerns, they'd need someone from law enforcement to help them bring down Vincent, and they couldn't do it without the information on the drive.

If they didn't find it, would Faith end up going to prison for a murder she didn't commit? Or worse… die at the hands of a man who had once been part of her family?

FIVE

Glimpses of the mountain jutted upward through the tall pines. They were almost to her former home. Though she couldn't see it, the familiar outcropping of rocks that hid the small farmhouse from view was there, along with an overflowing of memories. Both good and bad.

The woods she and Eli had traversed had been her and *Grossdaddi*'s playground. So many adventures had taken place here. *Grossdaddi* would explain about the different plants that grew in the forest. Many had medicinal powers.

All those years she'd lost with him and her grandmother for believing they were dead.

Forgiveness isn't for the guilty. It's for the wronged... Her grandmother's words came to mind.

For a long time, she'd resented her father for taking her from them, and it had almost destroyed her. After her parents' car accident, she'd struggled to forgive him. Maybe it was about time to let go of the past.

The rocks that concealed the homestead from anyone wandering through the woods came into view. As a child, she'd spend hours climbing them. Finding joy in the simple things. Living the Plain life to its fullest.

The past was all around her, pulling her back to that little girl she'd once been. She stopped walking. Things she hadn't thought about in years resurfaced from the place where she'd imprisoned them. No matter how hard she tried, she'd never understand why her father chose to walk away from this way of life.

Eli turned back to her with a frown on his face. "Did you hear something?"

She pulled in a shaky breath and fought against the resentment that had encased her heart for too long.

Let it go… Let God have it.

"No, nothing." She glanced over her shoulder before catching up with him.

Clearing the rocks, she watched the old homestead come into view. It was like going back in time. Little had changed through the years.

"That is a welcome sight," Eli said beside her. "I pray we will be safe here."

Grandmother Sarah must have been watching. As soon as they neared the house, she came out to them.

"Is everything *oke* at the house?" She looked between them.

Eli patted her arm. "*Jah*, everything is *oke*. The house is safe. Faith and I put out the fire. It shouldn't spread." He kept his arm around the elderly woman's shoulders as they returned to the house.

Eli placed the suitcase on the floor near the door and locked it before he closed the curtains.

"Is he gone?" Grandmother Sarah's worried eyes clamped on to Faith's.

She couldn't lie to her grandmother. "For now."

"But he will come back?"

Eli met Faith's gaze across the room. Saw her struggle to find an answer for her relative.

"We should be safe here. The house is hidden, and I will keep a careful watch. If he comes near the place, we'll know."

Sarah smiled at him. "You are right. We have you to protect us."

Faith hated putting such a burden on Eli. It wasn't fair. But she needed his help more than ever.

He patted Grandmother Sarah's arm but retained his attention on Faith. "We will be *oke*."

She smiled at the reminder of the strong young boy who'd looked after her as a child. Eli's protective instincts ran deep.

As they continued to watch each other across the space, something shifted in his eyes, and he cleared his throat and looked away. "It's cold in here. Let me get some wood from the shed and start the fire, then I'll take a look at your hand." He disappeared into the living room. Soon, a door opened and closed.

Faith glanced around her former family kitchen. Not much had changed through the years, though the place was showing signs of age. All her family's old furniture was where they'd left it. She stood near the table that her grandfather had given her mother as a wedding present and smoothed her hand across the surface. Nicks in the wood where the family had shared countless meals were still right here.

The good moments she'd shared here with her father returned. She'd almost forgotten about them. The way he made her mother laugh. And her. The times she'd walk into a room and find them hugging.

Once when she'd been about four or five and had woken to a thunderous clap outside her window. Terrified, Faith had run to her parents' room. Her dad had scooped her into his arms and held her until the storm passed.

She'd been so angry with him for leaving West Kootenai that she'd deliberately hidden the good times they'd shared.

"I miss them both," Grandmother Sarah whispered with a reminiscent look on her face.

She hugged this sweet woman. "Me too. Even though it's been years since the car accident, at times I still can't believe they're gone." She looked around the kitchen. "I loved living here so much. I'd almost forgotten how much until now."

Grandmother Sarah nodded with a sad smile on her face. "We have both lost so much. First, your grandfather, then your *daed* and *mamm*. Too much has been lost. We can't let this man take anything else from us."

"No, we can't," she said. Faith would do everything in her power to keep that from happening. She'd brought this nightmare to her grandmother, but she couldn't let Vincent hurt anyone else in her family. She wouldn't.

Eli came back inside and dumped wood on the floor. Seconds later he appeared in the kitchen doorway. Both women turned. When Faith looked at his face, she knew something was wrong.

"He found us," Faith said in a strangled voice.

Eli's troubled eyes met hers. "I believe so. After I gathered the wood, I looked around and spotted him walking through the woods past the road. I don't think he noticed me, but if he keeps coming this way, eventually he will spot the house."

Faith pulled her grandmother close. "What do we do?"

"Help me secure the doors in case he decides to break in like he did at Sarah's place. We should close the curtains, as well. Sarah, extinguish that lantern. If he thinks no one is home, perhaps he will leave."

Faith rushed to the sink and slid the curtains shut while Eli shoved a kitchen chair underneath the doorknob to secure it. Faith helped him heave the heavy wooden bookcase in front of the living room door. If Vincent broke down the door, the bookcase would at least slow him down. After she finished closing the rest of the curtains, Faith and Eli returned to the kitchen and waited.

The silence of the fading day was soon broken when someone stepped up on the front porch. Grandmother Sarah reached for Faith's arm and held it tightly.

A shadow moved across the porch to the door. Rattled it hard enough to shake the door on its hinges. Porch boards squeaked under the weight. A shadow appeared near the drawn curtains over the sink as if Vincent was trying to look inside.

Silence stretched on for a long period. The shadow appeared near the back door. Faith's nerves strung tighter when someone yanked on the doorknob several more times.

Grandmother Sarah's fearful eyes watched the door. Everyone in the room remained quiet. No one dared move. Soon footsteps left the porch and Faith breathed out a huge sigh and prayed Vincent had believed the place was empty.

Still, the reprieve would only be temporary. Vincent would search the rest of the property—every square inch of it—until he'd found her.

Should they take this chance to escape or wait it out? The ruthless way Vincent had burned the structure to the ground knowing they were inside kept playing through Eli's head.

He had no idea how much time had passed but it seemed like forever. His mind raced about what to do next. They couldn't stay hidden inside the house like this forever.

"I'm going to check outside," he told Faith at last. "Stay here with your grandmother."

He started to leave the room, but she caught his arm. "Eli, no. It's too dangerous. He knows you."

The worry on her face was for Eli alone and so undeserved by him. While he wished to reassure her everything would be alright, he wasn't anywhere close to believing it for himself.

"Stay here with Sarah," he said and untangled her hand from his arm. "I'll be right *oke.*"

Faith handed him his jacket, and Eli moved to the living room and inched the curtains apart. Nothing out of the ordinary appeared as far as he could see. But Vincent was out there somewhere.

Eli continued through the rest of the house searching windows. Where had the man gone?

He grabbed the shotgun and removed the chair from beneath the doorknob. Easing the kitchen door open, he slipped outside and listened as the quiet of the place settled around him.

Muddy footsteps covered the porch. Eli flattened

himself against the wall and edged toward the side facing the barn. Right away he witnessed a chilling reminder of what happened at Sarah's. The barn door stood wide open. So far, none of the animals were loose. As much as he wanted to rush over and close it, not knowing where Vincent was hiding held him back.

Sticking close to the house, he stopped short when he glimpsed Vincent's truck through the trees. Eli jerked out of sight. Was Vincent inside the truck? While he thought about the best plan to get them out of this dangerous situation, footsteps tromped through the trees between the front of the house and the road.

Eli made sure Vincent wasn't nearby before he moved toward the closest tree. Once he reached it, he steadied his breathing and peeked around the side. A group of lodgepole pines obscured his visual, but he didn't see anyone. Had Vincent slipped past him and headed for the house?

Panic threatened to overtake him. He'd left Faith and Sarah all alone. Eli ran for the house while moving from tree to tree to stay out of sight, his breath pumping from his chest. Mind whirling with all his past failures. He'd failed Miriam. Now those who trusted him were vulnerable.

Faith's face peeked through a sliver in the curtain. She pointed at something behind him. Eli dove for the closest tree.

Crack! A gunshot pierced the silence. He'd been seconds away from dying. If Faith hadn't warned him…

"You thought you could outsmart me?" Vincent huffed breaths.

Eli edged away from the tree in time to see the

deadly intent in Vincent's eyes as he prepared to fire again.

Ducking quickly, Eli narrowly avoided the next bullet that lodged near where his head had been seconds earlier. Vincent wasn't letting up, and he'd never make it back to the house like this.

Eli raised the shotgun to fire. Vincent had closed the space between them and was inches away. Eli squeezed the trigger, but Vincent knocked the shotgun barrel away with his hand. The shot flew past Vincent's shoulder as he hit Eli full speed. Both went flying backward onto the ground. Eli lost the weapon in the process.

Vincent grabbed hold of his jacket and slammed his fist into Eli's jaw. His head struck the ground. The rage on Vincent's face was all he saw. Eli shoved Vincent hard enough to get him off, then jumped to his feet and searched for the shotgun that had flown from his hand.

It had landed near one of the trees. Before he had time to grab it, Vincent was standing and aiming the weapon at Eli's head. With no other choice, Eli threw his body at the man and somehow managed to keep his feet beneath him when Vincent slugged him again and tried to get the weapon into a position to shoot.

Eli grabbed for the gun and struggled with all his might to free it while Vincent fought just as hard to kill him.

A noise nearby sounded over the battle raging between them. Vincent's head flew up and he listened. Eli took advantage and shoved hard. Vincent stumbled backward, but his attention was focused on something behind Eli.

Eli whirled in time to see Faith pull the trigger on

the shotgun. The bullet seared through Vincent's shoulder. He screamed and grabbed his injured arm.

Before Faith had time to reload, Vincent took off toward the truck at a fast pace.

Stunned, Eli watched the man disappear and couldn't believe what happened.

Vincent had somehow figured out that they weren't dead and had come looking for them. Now he knew where they were hiding. He'd keep coming. And the next time the outcome might be far more deadly.

SIX

"Eli!" Faith ran to his side. "Are you okay?" The side of his reddened face where Vincent had struck him had begun to swell.

"I am, but this man is not giving up." He looked straight at her. "And we are no match for him."

Faith was shaking all over and couldn't help it. She picked up Eli's black felt hat from where it had fallen and dusted it off before handing it to him. Because of her, Eli had almost lost his life. And he was right. Vincent wouldn't let up. He wasn't even trying to pretend any longer that this was about bringing her in for a crime. He was here to kill her and anyone else who might get in the way of his freedom.

She clasped his chin and turned him with a gentle touch to examine his injured cheek. He winced and jerked away.

"I'm so sorry," she said. "I never meant to pull you into my troubles." This wasn't what she wanted. So many people had gotten hurt because of her. First Cheryl. Now Eli and her grandmother. All because of Vincent's and Blake's crimes.

Eli reached for her wrist and turned her hand up so

that he looked at the red burn marks. "You have nothing to be sorry for. Nothing at all. This isn't your fault."

She smiled sadly. "But it is. All of it. And you're right—it's time to speak with the sheriff. There are more lives at stake besides mine. Vincent must be stopped." She heaved a sigh. Every time she thought about Cheryl's murder, it was like a nail drove through her heart.

"We'll do it together. I will go with you. I am told the sheriff is a fair man."

The relief she felt at hearing him say this was priceless. "Thank you, Eli, but I have to try one more time to find the drive."

His expression softened. "Of course." The sincerity in his eyes had been there so many times in the past. Now it tugged her back in time. Awoke feelings that she thought she would never experience again after Blake's betrayal. "We'll take Sarah and go there together."

She shivered and the ticking clock in her head warned their time was almost up. She glanced around the homestead that had once been her family's. "I don't want Grandmother to be part of what's happening any more than she already has been. Is there someplace safe she can stay while we speak with the sheriff?"

Eli didn't hesitate. "There is. My *bruder*'s home is not far from *Mamm*'s. Aaron will help us."

The thought of bringing someone else into this dangerous situation was the last thing she wanted, but what other choice did she have?

"Okay." She slowly pulled her gaze from his. Amid so much danger and uncertainty, something unexpected was happening and she wasn't sure she could trust her instincts again. She'd believed Blake was a good man who would never hurt her.

Faith dragged in several breaths and tried to think beyond her emotions. Her sweet grandmother watched them from the window. Faith couldn't imagine how frightened she must be.

Eli let her go and stepped back, his breathing as unsteady as hers. "The wagon is still at Sarah's, but I have my buggy in the barn and my older mare. She can pull it. I'll get the buggy ready to travel. There is some salve for your burns in the kitchen cabinet. Can you and Sarah treat them?"

With all that had happened, she'd almost forgotten the burns. While they weren't serious, they might slow her down if left untreated.

"Of course," she said, moved by his concern for her after everything he'd gone through.

Eli slowly nodded. "Good. There are extra jackets by the door. One for you and one for Sarah. It's getting colder by the minute. You will need them for warmth. We won't be able to take the road. I have no doubt he'll be waiting for us to make that move. Taking the buggy through the thick trees will be difficult, but Vincent shouldn't be able to get his massive truck in to follow us."

"I'll get Grandmother Sarah, and we'll meet you in the barn soon."

As they continued to watch each other without moving, Faith pulled in an unsteady breath. Lost in his eyes, it was easy to forget the danger facing them. That time was critical.

Eli responded, then started for the barn. She couldn't take her eyes off him. This handsome man was working his way into her heart, and she wasn't ready to let him in. Could she let him in?

Faith turned toward the road. The day was fading and they wouldn't have much time to search for the drive before nightfall.

She hurried up the steps of the porch and the door opened. Grandmother Sarah had been watching for her.

"I saw that man attack Eli." The worry on her grandmother's face was crushing. "If you hadn't fired at him when you did…"

Faith came inside, closed the door and relocked it. "We are both *oke*, but we can't stay here and wait for him to come back." She hurried to the kitchen and found the salve Eli mentioned along with some gauze. She smeared the salve on the burns then waited while her grandmother wrapped it.

"Let's get your suitcase," she said once they were finished. "We're leaving as soon as Eli gets the buggy ready."

Her grandmother picked up the suitcase from where they'd left it earlier.

"Where will we go?" Grandmother asked in a worried tone as they headed toward the front of the house.

Faith handed her one of the jackets and slipped into the second one.

"Eli is taking you to his brother's place while he and I go to speak with the sheriff. You will be safe there." She hoped it proved true.

Faith explained they would be stopping along the way to look for the drive once more.

Outside, a horse snorted. Faith parted the curtains and looked out in time to see him guiding a horse and buggy to the porch.

Somewhere out there, Vincent was lurking. Licking his wounds. Regrouping. Preparing for the next attack.

She had a feeling Vincent would not let a little thing like a gunshot stand in his way.

Faith opened the door and ushered her grandmother down the steps. Eli stowed the suitcase and helped them both into the buggy.

He eased the horse behind the house. "We should be safe enough going through the woods, but we'll have to steer clear of any place where Vincent may be able to ambush us, though."

The weather had continued to grow colder with the lengthening shadows, yet much more than the cold burrowed down into Faith's bones. A fear that wouldn't go away had her watching each passing tree as if she expected Vincent to jump out from behind one.

Faith tugged the jacket closely around her body. The gathering darkness had turned the woods to night.

"I have battery-powered lights on the buggy, but I don't think it's wise to use them. We would be giving away our location."

She was glad Eli was thinking for them. Lack of sleep was inhibiting her from keeping her thoughts together.

The fading daylight wouldn't lend itself to finding the drive, but what choice did she have? She didn't believe Vincent had it yet, but if he managed to find the drive, nothing would stop him from ending her.

Eli covered her hand with his. "If it's still there, we'll do our best to locate it."

She smiled despite the circumstances and took comfort in having him at her side. Eli would do everything in his power to help her bring Vincent to justice. She prayed it would be enough.

As they continued through the silty darkness in the woods, the only sounds were the mare's breathing and Faith's racing pulse drumming against her ears. Letting go of her fears wasn't possible until Vincent was no longer a threat.

In the distance, river sounds overtook the mare's breathing. They were close to the water.

"There it is." Eli nodded up ahead. The mare grew skittish as they neared, and Eli stopped her some distance away.

As much as Faith hated having her grandmother out in the open like this, the river was closer to Grandmother Sarah's house than it was to Aaron's place, which was halfway across the community, according to Eli.

Eli hopped down and tied off the mare while they climbed out.

"Careful. It's slippery." Faith interlocked her arm with Grandmother Sarah's, and they picked their way down the bank.

"I'll search across the creek." Eli pointed to a spot on the opposite side. "There's a downed tree where I can get across. You and Sarah should stay where I can see you both." Though he didn't say as much, she believed he was thinking about what happened the last time they'd been here.

"We'll start here," she told him. "With the current running this strong, it could be anywhere."

Inches away, Eli held her gaze for a moment, and everything but the man before her disappeared.

She chewed her bottom lip. Why did she feel this

connection to Eli? They hadn't seen each other in years. Was it the past and happier times creeping into this moment of vulnerability? Before she could pin the truth into place, Eli started for the tree that had fallen across the creek, and she let go of an unsteady breath.

Her grandmother had witnessed the moment shared between Faith and Eli. What must she be thinking?

"Let's start over there," Faith said without looking at her grandmother. She pointed to the spot where they hadn't searched yet. "The drive is in a plastic ziplock bag. Since Vincent didn't appear to know about the drive, it must have fallen out when my purse opened. Before he found the purse." She glanced around them. "I know it's a long shot, but I need it if I'm going to convince the sheriff I'm telling the truth."

Grandmother Sarah grabbed her arm when Faith would have moved away. She turned toward this sweet lady.

"It will be *oke*, child. *Gott* will not let you suffer for this man's crimes. He sees all. He will keep you safe."

Despite the circumstances, she smiled. Faith had heard her say that same thing many times while she was growing up. Her grandmother was a woman of strong faith who put her trust in God and refused to let anything, no matter how difficult, shake that foundation.

When the trouble between Faith's father and grandfather reached a breaking point, her grandmother spent many an hour on her knees praying for God to intervene. But that hadn't happened, and everything in their lives had changed.

"*Gott* will hear, child. He answers in His own way. His own time."

Faith wished she shared that same steadfastness, but if life had taught her anything, it was that the only person she could count on was herself.

Darkness descended little by little until there was very little light left to see. There'd been no sign of the drive so far and Eli had a sinking feeling it was lost for good. Every second they were out here like this, there was a chance they would be spotted by Vincent.

He returned to the women. Faith glanced up as he approached.

"We shouldn't stay here any longer. It's too dangerous."

The disappointment on her face was hard to take.

"I know." She scanned the water where the car's roof just broke the surface. "I pray it's at the bottom of the creek. At least there it will be out of Vincent's reach."

Eli held on to Sarah's arm and helped her along the uneven path while Faith kept close. As they neared the spot where he'd left the buggy, he stopped short as a prickling of danger slithered into his stomach.

Seeing through the pitch black was difficult. As his eyes adjusted more to the deeper woods, something caught his attention. The buggy was where they'd left it, but the mare was gone.

Vincent. He'd been here and unharnessed the animal.

"Hurry!" Eli grabbed hold of Faith and Sarah and raced through the woods.

They'd taken only a handful of steps when a terrifying sound drowned out his labored breathing. Rapid gunfire.

"Stay low!" Eli yelled over the noise and didn't let go of their hands.

The road came into view. Silence permeated the woods.

While Eli tried to come up with a way to escape the man coming after them, the quiet evaporated into another round of gunfire. Bullets peppered the trees all around them. One struck Eli's right shoulder. Hot lead and pain drilled a hole through his flesh. He struggled to keep his footing.

"Eli!" Faith screamed when he dropped her hand and grabbed his shoulder.

"Keep going," he said through gritted teeth. If they stopped, they'd die in these woods.

The road opened in front of them. Vincent's truck stood parked off the shoulder.

"Over there." Faith pointed to the truck. "If the keys are in it, we can get use it to get away."

The pain in his shoulder had begun to trickle down his arm. Through his body. He was fading quickly.

Faith wrapped her arm around his waist while her grandmother did the same, and they helped him to the truck. Behind them, Vincent stormed through the trees at a fast pace.

She opened the driver's door and looked inside. "Nothing." Had she been wrong? She remembered Blake sometimes left his keys above the visor whenever he planned to return to his vehicle soon.

"Can you stand on your own?" Eli managed a semblance of a nod but could see her doubts. "Hold on to him," she told her grandmother. As soon as Faith loosened her grip, he swayed and reached for the truck bed.

While he watched, Faith flipped down the driver's

side visor. Still nothing. "The driver's fender," she exclaimed and dipped out of sight.

Seconds passed while he looked behind them expecting Vincent to appear at any moment.

"Thank You, God." Faith held up the key.

With Sarah's help, they got Eli inside the vehicle. He leaned heavily against the closed door. Sarah slipped in beside him and Faith started the vehicle.

"Oh, no," she said when Vincent emerged from the trees behind them.

Faith pressed down on the gas pedal and the truck sped away.

Eli watched the side mirror. Vincent was running after them with the gun waving wildly. "Get down, Sarah." He urged the woman out of sight. Vincent unloaded his weapon into the back of the truck.

Faith never slowed down. The truck swerved on the slick road, and she fought to control it.

Vincent ran after them, shooting until they were out of range.

Faith's attention flew to Eli. "I'm *oke*," he murmured, but the words were jumbled. He didn't even know if they were clear. "We need to get out of sight now."

"You've lost a lot of blood, Eli, but we can't afford to stop until we're away from Vincent's danger." Her sweet voice drifted his way. So full of promises. If only he deserved those promises.

"Grandmother, can you use your prayer *kapp* to put pressure on the wound for now?" Faith's worried gaze blurred before Eli's eyes and he closed them.

"Eli, stay with me." Her voice rose an octave.

"I will." He thought he said it aloud but couldn't be sure.

Sarah applied gentle pressure against his wounded arm, a reminder that there were many people who cared for him. Just as many he'd let down. His family. Mason. His *fraa*. Now Faith and Sarah. He thought he was making the right choice by heading to the creek to search for the drive, but instead, he'd almost cost them all their lives.

"I'm sorry," he murmured. "Sorry, Miriam." His wife's face drifted in his mind. Someone shook him. He opened his eyes and saw the worry etched on Faith's face. All for him. "I let you down," he mumbled.

"No, you didn't. You saved us. And I'm not going to let anything happen to you, so stay with me, Eli. Stay focused on me."

He forced his heavy eyes to remain open and held his attention on her pretty face while wondering how anyone could hurt someone like her. He'd done his best to protect her. He would always try to protect her.

"Which way to Aaron's?" A frown line appeared between her brows. He struggled to stay alert.

Eli rousted himself and looked behind them. Nothing but blackness. "He's not there."

Faith's full attention was on the road ahead. "No, that's right, he's not back there. We have the advantage because we have his vehicle." Her attention went briefly to Sarah, who continued to hold pressure against his arm, and then back to the road.

Eli sucked in a breath, winced and stared out the windshield. "Aaron lives on the other side of the community. To get there, you will need to get off this road. There's a path coming up on your left, past the com-

munity shops." He frowned and tried to hold on to
his thoughts, but the blood loss was taking its toll. He
could feel himself slowing down.

With Vincent still on the loose, they'd be in danger every mile of the long drive to Eagle's Nest and
the sheriff's office there. He didn't want to put Sarah
through that ordeal after everything she'd gone through
so far. She would be safe at Aaron's home and he
wouldn't have to worry about her. "It's not very well
kept. I'm not sure the truck will make it through."

Faith chewed her bottom lip. "We don't have a
choice."

He understood what she meant, but if the truck got
stuck, they'd have a long walk ahead of them and he
wasn't sure he was up to it.

"There it is." Sarah pointed to the narrow opening
barely visible through overgrown trees.

Faith stopped close to the entrance and stared at it
with doubts. "We don't have a choice," she repeated to
herself and eased the truck into the space.

Potholes formed from recent weather slung the truck
all around. Eli slammed against the door and grabbed
his shoulder.

Faith slowed to a crawl and glanced his way. "I'm
sorry. I'll try not to do that again."

She steered the truck through a series of holes big
enough to break a buggy wheel. Eli gripped the bottom
of the seat and did his best to keep from being sick.
His pulse pounded through his veins and down his
wounded shoulder. It hummed a rhythm that seemed
to chime, *a long way to go before the nightmare ends*.
A long way before they were safe.

SEVEN

The truck lurched along the rough road. Faith gripped the wheel with both hands but it was a battle even at the slow speed.

"How much farther?" she asked and glanced over to where Eli had slumped against the door. "Eli!" She braked the vehicle and shook him.

His eyes popped open. He said something she couldn't understand.

Putting the truck in Park, Faith grabbed the gauze she'd stuffed in her jacket and found an old T-shirt. She hopped out and went around to Eli's door. Her grandmother's white prayer *kapp* was now bloodred, but by putting pressure on the wound she had slowed down the blood loss.

"Try to relax, Eli. Help me get his jacket off," she said to her grandmother. With the older woman's assistance, they eased the jacket from Eli's shoulders. He winced from even the smallest of movements.

"I'm sorry—I know it hurts." As a nurse at one of the busiest hospitals in New York, Faith had seen many gunshot victims, but she'd never witnessed a shooting until she'd watched Cheryl die at the hands of her husband. And now Eli had been shot by this ruthless man.

Once the jacket had been removed, Faith unbuttoned his shirt and moved it away from the wound so she could get a good look at what she was dealing with.

Her fingers felt around the back side of Eli's shoulder until she found a wound where the bullet had exited.

She used part of the gauze to wipe blood away while Eli clamped his lips together. The glazed look in his eyes was one she'd witnessed many times.

All her fault. The truth repeated through her mind, an unwelcome thought.

Faith secured the wound as best she could. With her grandmother's help, she eased his shirt back into place. "That should stop the bleeding for now. We need to keep moving."

Eli reached for her hand before she moved away, saw the bloodstains there. His eyes latched on to hers. She wished things could be different.

"Rest now," she said, then tugged her hand free and stepped back. Pulling in a shaky breath, she closed the door and circled the back of the truck. Her mind went over all the conversations she'd had with Eli, replaying everything that happened between them. He'd been her protector since she was a little girl. Had always been part of her life. Through the years, she'd thought a lot about her life here. Her grandparents. Eli.

Foolish... Her life was in shambles. She was the target of a man who would stop at nothing to silence her. She had to stay focused.

She got behind the wheel without looking Eli's way, put the truck into Drive and eased down the path.

As she fought to keep the truck from bottoming out in places, the missing drive kept popping into her thoughts. If Vincent discovered it, her only play was gone. He would want to tie up all loose ends, which meant he'd have her grandmother and Eli killed along with her. The sooner they had the chance to speak with the sheriff, the better. She just hoped he would believe her.

"If you take the next turnoff coming up, my *bruder*'s home will be down that way." Eli's thread of a voice interrupted her troubled thoughts, and she glanced his way. His eyes were closed. Complexion pale.

The road he spoke of appeared, and Faith turned onto it. After they'd traveled some distance along the relatively smooth path, Grandmother Sarah pointed to another turnoff coming up. "That one runs in front of Aaron's home."

Faith smiled her way while casting a worried look to what appeared to be an unconscious Eli.

"He will be *oke*. Eli is a strong man."

But he hadn't been shot before. She chose not to share that with her grandmother.

With her attention on the road ahead, she couldn't get to Aaron's house quickly enough. Though they'd escaped Vincent tonight, this was far from over. Leaving the truck at Aaron's house wasn't a good idea.

"That's Aaron's home."

Faith's attention went to the house on the left. It was typical of so many other Amish homes. White clapboard siding. A wooden fence separated the property from the road. The house set some distance away.

She didn't remember much about Aaron from their childhoods, but her grandmother had told her Aaron's wife, Irene, had passed away a few years back. He'd recently remarried.

As she slowed enough to turn onto the drive, Eli woke with the rocking movement. He glanced around with confusion in his eyes.

"We're at your brother's house," Faith told him.

As they neared the house, a man stepped out onto the porch holding a lantern high. He clamped his black hat down over dark hair. His resemblance to Eli was clear.

Faith stopped the truck and opened the door. After climbing out, she went around to help Eli from the vehicle. As soon as Aaron saw his injured brother, he hurried down the steps.

"Eli, what has happened?" The concern etched on Aaron's face was clear in the lantern's glow.

Eli did his best to explain.

"Let's get you inside." Aaron grabbed his brother around the waist and helped him inside while Faith and Grandmother Sarah followed.

Once they reached the door, Faith glanced back at the road they'd just traveled. Darkness covered the community. The countryside appeared peaceful, but nothing could be further from the truth. As a cop, Vincent would have a way of using the truck's GPS to find the missing vehicle. He'd be tracking them, but with Eli injured there was no way he could have walked the entire distance to Aaron's house.

Still, they'd have to move the truck quickly and as far away from Aaron's house as possible. Before Vincent found them. Because somewhere out there he waited, plotting his next desperate move.

* * *

Eli's shoulder felt much better after Faith's gentle care, but his mind wouldn't let him relax. Even though they were safe for now, and Aaron's wife, Victoria, was a former trained CIA agent, he couldn't get Vincent out of his head. The man appeared unstoppable.

Victoria brought over a cup of *kaffe* to take the chill away.

"Denki." Eli smiled at his sister-in-law. He'd liked her from the moment they met.

Victoria nodded, but he could see there was something troubling her. "I can ride to the phone shanty and reach out to one of my former colleagues." She looked him in the eye. "They will be able to help."

"That may be our next move, but first we try to reach the sheriff."

Aaron spoke highly of Sheriff Collins. Eli believed they could trust the law enforcement officer.

Victoria nodded. "Anything I can do to help." She hesitated and he dreaded what she was about to say. "I hate to be the bearer of more bad news, but if this man has gone to such extremes to find you, then he won't let a little thing like not having a vehicle stop him from continuing to search for you." She glanced from Eli to Faith. "There's a good chance he may be able to tap into the truck's GPS system. If he does, he'll track it here."

The idea horrified Eli.

"She's right," Faith said with a nod. "We have to move it. I'll take the truck off somewhere and leave it. Someplace far from here so he can't trace it back to you and Aaron."

"I can come with you," Victoria offered, and Aaron clasped his wife's hand.

"Do you forget you are having a baby?" The gentle smile on his *bruder*'s face was all for his wife. "I'll go with Faith."

Aaron's *sohn*, Caleb, rose. "*Daed*, let me." Young Caleb would be starting his *rumspringa* soon enough.

He headed for the shotgun near the door, but Eli stopped him. "I will go with Faith."

Faith rejected the idea immediately. "You're not strong enough. You've been shot, Eli."

He got to his feet and tried not to wobble. "I am fine. If its *oke* with you, *bruder*, I'll take the buggy and follow Faith. That way, we can ride back together."

Aaron readily agreed. "But you should let me come with you for added protection."

Eli appreciated his *bruder*'s desire to help, but he couldn't accept the offer. He shook his head. "*Nay*. Stay here with your family and Sarah."

Aaron agreed. "Alright. Stay here where it's warm. I'll get the buggy ready." He patted Eli's arm and grabbed his coat. With Caleb at his side, Aaron removed the lantern from the peg near the door and headed out into the night.

"Are you sure it is wise for you and Faith to go alone?" Sarah asked Eli.

She was worried, with good reason, and he struggled to reassure her. "The fewer people involved, the better. I'll take Aaron's weapon for added protection. Faith can use my shotgun. We'll be safe enough."

Yet Sarah's worry didn't ease, and Victoria placed her arm around the older woman. "They will be alright."

When he'd come home, Aaron had told him about the nightmare Victoria had gone through when she arrived in West Kootenai. The former CIA agent had been hunted by men who wanted to silence her, much like Vincent did Faith.

The buggy approached the house. Eli eased into his torn jacket and tugged on his hat.

"Take *Daed*'s gun with you, *Onkel* Eli." Caleb handed him the shotgun and a box of shells. Eli smiled at his nephew. He'd gotten to know Caleb while the young man had begun learning the logging part of the family business. He was smart and caught on quickly. The family furniture and logging business would be in *gut* hands when Caleb took over one day.

"*Denki*, Caleb." With Faith at his side, they stepped from the warmth of the house into the cold night.

Aaron headed up the steps. "There's no sign of anyone on the road, but if he's still on foot, it will be hard to know where he's at until it's too late."

"We will be careful, *bruder*," Eli assured him.

"The best place to leave the truck is on the opposite side of the community away from Silver Creek," Aaron told Faith. "It is a less-traveled path."

"Thank you. For everything." She faced Eli. "Are you ready?"

"Jah." He headed down the steps. With Faith's help, he made it up to the bench seat. Eli placed the shotgun at his feet so it would be close enough to reach at a second's notice. "Let me lead the way," he told her and glanced up at the clearing skies. "There should be enough light from the stars to see where we're going. Keep off your headlights. We don't want to draw attention to ourselves."

She started toward the truck. Once it was running,

Eli guided Aaron's gelding to the drive while Faith crept along behind him.

Eli's shoulder ached with each jostle of the buggy. He wasn't anywhere close to being 100 percent and hoped there wouldn't be another run-in with Vincent.

At the end of the drive, he turned left onto the road. With Faith close behind him, they inched their way toward the edge of the community. It was slow going that seemed to take forever to reach the place Aaron suggested.

A small logging trail came into view. Eli pulled the buggy off the road and indicated Faith should take the truck farther down the trail.

She turned onto the trail and he followed. Once she'd traveled far enough to be out of sight from the main road, Faith drove off into the woods and got out. With a final glance at the truck, she hurried to the buggy and climbed up beside him.

The gelding responded easily to his command to turn around the buggy. Eli headed back toward the street. Being out in the open had his nerves on edge. With his heart in his throat, Eli pulled onto the road.

"How's your shoulder?" Faith asked when she noticed the way he favored it.

Eli sought to reassure her although the wound hurt terribly. "Better, thanks to you."

She rubbed her hands across her arms. "Not thanks to me. This is all my fault."

He wouldn't let her take on blame for something she couldn't have foreseen. "*Nay.* You are just as much a victim as Cheryl. She can no longer speak for herself. You must tell her story. Must make sure this man is held accountable for what he did to her and to your husband. The others."

She searched his face before she slowly smiled. It lifted some of the weariness around her eyes. Her smile made everything they'd gone through worth the cost. Faith was *gut* person who'd gotten involved with someone who wasn't.

As they continued along the road, a car crested the hill in front of them still some distance away. Eli sat up straighter and tried to see the vehicle beyond the headlights but couldn't. Still, at this time of the evening on a road rarely traveled by *Englischers*, this wasn't some strange coincidence.

Faith grabbed his arm. The headlights would pick up the buggy soon enough. While Eli didn't understand the *Englischers'* technology, the tension tying his gut into knots seemed to warn that they were in big trouble. "We have to get off the road before he picks us up in the headlights."

And that wouldn't take long. Their only option was to head off into the woods near the road.

Eli clicked his tongue and directed the horse from the road. The animal balked, then climbed the embankment with ease.

There was barely enough time to get off the street before the car passed. Eli strained to see the driver, but the cabin was unusually dark.

"Whoa." Eli stopped the horse and turned to Faith. "Were you able to see who was driving?"

She shook her head. "No, it was too dark inside."

Eli handed her the reins and hopped from the buggy. "I'm going to walk down a little way to see if it turns onto the road where we left the truck. If so, then I'd say there's no doubt that it's Vincent."

Faith got down beside him and tied the reins to a nearby tree. "I'm going with you."

"That's unwise." He stepped closer. "You know what this man is capable of."

"I do. That's why I'm coming with you."

Her concern for him was touching. She was a caring woman who hadn't deserved any of what was happening to her.

Eli retrieved his shotgun and handed it to Faith, then loaded Aaron's and shoved the extra shells into his coat pocket.

"We stay in the trees," he told her while his racing heart sent him jumping at every little noise.

Faith glued herself to his side as they started through the woods.

The road where the truck was parked came into view. There was no sign of the car. Had the driver kept going?

Eli breathed out a sigh. "I don't see the car." He looked toward Faith. Instead of relief, the expression on her face was pure horror. Her huge eyes stared at something behind him.

He whirled around with a sinking feeling. Vincent stood a few feet away with a leer on his face and a gun in his hand.

EIGHT

"I knew that was you two I saw on the road," Vincent said as he closed the limited space between them without lowering his weapon. Before Faith had time to react, Vincent snatched the gun from her hand and then pointed his at her head. "Toss that weapon over to me now," he told Eli. "Before I shoot her right where she's standing."

"Don't do it, Eli," Faith warned. If Eli gave up his weapon, they'd be completely defenseless, and she was positive Vincent planned to kill them.

Vincent fired a shot above her head. "Next one won't miss."

Eli slowly tossed the gun at Vincent's feet. Faith edged closer to him and reached for his hand. He made her feel safe, and she believed after everything they'd been through—the things that happened in New York—*Gott* wouldn't let them die like this.

While keeping a close eye on them, Vincent picked up both weapons and hurled them into the underbrush.

With the gun still trained on them, Vincent moved closer. A triumphant grin played across his face. "This could have been avoided if you'd kept what Blake told you to yourself. Instead, you had to blab it to Cheryl. Now this guy and that old woman. Look what's happened because you couldn't keep your mouth shut." He waved the gun in her face and winced. Vincent appeared to be favoring his injured shoulder. Their only chance at getting through this would be finding a way to disarm Vincent.

"Let's go!" he barked and they jumped. "You're both coming with me."

Vincent pointed toward the road. "Get going!" His expression twisted into rage when they hesitated. He shoved Eli's injured arm, and Eli bit back his reaction to the pain. "Go." Faith started toward Eli, but Vincent grabbed her by the arm and hauled her along with him toward the truck.

If they got into that vehicle with Vincent, they'd be dead. He'd probably take them somewhere off the community and shoot them. Maybe into the mountains where he'd leave their bodies for the animals to dispose of. Faith couldn't let that happen. Eli was right. She had to tell Cheryl's story. To do so, she had to survive.

Vincent dragged her along beside him, then crossed the road and headed for the truck.

The closer they came to their fate, the more frantic she became. "I made copies of all the evidence Blake gathered. If I go missing, it'll be sent to someone with enough authority to bring down you and the rest of your dirty cop friends along with Ghost."

Vincent jerked her to face him. "You're bluffing. You have nothing. And my wife's body is still in your house. You fled the scene of a murder."

His eyes narrowed as he watched her. "That really doesn't look good for you. I'll tell them I was forced to kill you both in self-defense. And the old lady won't be of much help. I know where she lives. I'll make sure she's taken care of next."

Faith tried not to take the bait no matter how hard it was. Aaron and his wife would protect her grandmother.

Out of the corner of her eye, Faith noticed Eli reaching inside the bed of the truck. She had to keep Vincent talking and distracted.

"You're wrong. The evidence is on its way to the FBI as we speak, along with the recording." She held Vincent's gaze. Saw a glint of doubt and pressed on. "I told them where to find you. They'll be coming soon. If I were you, I'd get out of here while you still can."

He jerked her to within a few inches of his face. Anger radiated from his pores. "What recording?" Facing her, Vincent didn't realize that Eli, who had a bat concealed behind his back, was slowly advancing.

"The one I recorded of you at the creek confessing to killing Cheryl and Blake. You had no idea I was taping you, did you?"

He shoved the weapon against her temple. Faith stifled a scream. Eli raised the bat. She closed her eyes and prayed his attack would be in time to save her.

The bat made contact. In an instant, she was freed. Her eyes opened and she stumbled away in time to see Vincent hit the ground.

Eli dropped the bat and grabbed Vincent's weapon, then her hand. "Let's go. I didn't hit him all that hard. We won't have long before he wakes up and when he does, he'll be madder than ever."

They ran toward the main road, crossed it, and kept going.

All Faith could think of was how she'd been seconds from dying. The sensation of the cold barrel against her temple remained strong.

Once they reached the buggy, Eli retrieved their weapons and quickly untied the reins while Faith scrambled onto the seat. When Eli was beside her, he didn't waste time getting the gelding headed through the sparse woods as fast as possible under the conditions.

They traveled for a long while before either spoke.

"Are you *oke*?" Eli asked and looked her over.

She wasn't—far from it. She couldn't stop shaking.

Though she was never close to Vincent, Faith and Blake had spent holidays and other special occasions with him and Cheryl. All the while she had no idea about the monster that lurked beneath the surface. Or the secret Vincent and her husband held on to.

Something Cheryl said came to mind. At the time, Faith had wondered if it was a joke, but there'd been something in Cheryl's eyes that said different. They'd gone out for a late movie when both their husbands were working. Afterward, they'd had coffee.

She and Cheryl were finishing their drinks when Vincent called. Right away, Cheryl's demeanor changed. She joked about getting home before Vincent killed her. That troubling look on her face had haunted Faith for a long time afterward. When Faith had asked Cheryl what she meant, she'd tried to downplay it by saying they'd had an argument.

After he'd killed her friend, Faith kept remembering the times Cheryl had bruises on her arm yet excused the injuries as clumsiness.

"His wife was my best friend. We spent the holidays together. How could I not see the truth about him?"

"He is *gut* at hiding his true self. That's how he got away with the crimes he's committed for so long."

She shifted toward him. He was a good man who had suffered the loss of his wife and she'd been so focused on staying alive that she hadn't thought to ask him about his life.

There were many things she didn't know about Eli, but she wanted to.

Faith touched his arm. "I'm so sorry to hear about your wife, Eli," she said in a gentle tone. "How did she die?"

His body tensed and he didn't look at her for the longest time. "She died in a fire two years ago."

Faith had no idea the depth of pain he'd had to live with. "Eli, I'm so sorry. What was her name?"

He turned his head toward her. "Miriam. She moved here after you left West Kootenai. She has family here still. Willa, her sister, is close to your age, and her *mamm* lives here, though she has been ill for a while."

He pulled in a breath. "Miriam and I married at seventeen. We moved away to the Libby community and lived there for many years." He stopped speaking. Didn't look at her.

"Oh, Eli." She touched his hand.

His broken look reached out to her. They were kindred spirits. Both had lost so much.

"She was my everything, and she died in a fire because I wasn't there to save her."

Faith couldn't keep her surprise to herself. "I'm sure you did everything you could."

Before she even finished, he shook his head. "I

wasn't there. I was working at a logging camp. Miriam needed me, but I was more concerned about making money than being there for her."

She didn't believe that for a moment. "You were doing what was necessary to provide."

His laugh held a derisive air. "That's what I told myself, but I enjoyed the extra money my *Englisch* employer paid me. The more hours I worked, the more money I made." He shook his head. "I was supposed to come home the night of the fire, but I was tired and decided to go home in the morning. So, I spent the night in one of the bunkhouses set up for workers. I was sleeping while Miriam died." He shook his head. "The fire department said the fire was set deliberately. Someone came into our house and started it."

She struggled to take it all in. "Did they catch the person?" He was silent for so long that she regretted asking. "I'm sorry. It's none of my business."

"They believed I set the fire," he said in such a soft voice that she almost didn't hear him. The hurt in his eyes was hard to take.

"But you were at the logging camp." She would never believe Eli was capable of such a thing.

"The camp wasn't that far from our home. No one there remembered seeing me during the time frame when the fire was started. The police were called in to investigate. They brought me in for questioning. Told me they were certain I was responsible for my wife's death and they planned to prove it."

A sliver of apprehension sped up her spine. Vincent threatened to frame her for Cheryl's death to destroy her credibility. She understood what it felt like to be accused of something you didn't do.

"But you didn't do anything wrong. The truth will come out." She wanted to believe that for Eli and for herself.

He stared straight ahead. "Miriam and I were going to have a child. I thought if I worked harder, I could provide better for my family. But she'd asked me to come home. Something was troubling her. She needed me, and I let her down. If only I'd listened to my *fraa* and not been so caught up in making money, Miriam may still be alive."

She had to make him understand that if he had been home the consequences of the evening might have been far different. "If you had gone home, you would be dead, as well."

He managed a tiny smile, but she could tell he didn't believe her.

Eli had lost so much. Like her, he was a troubled soul caught up in circumstances beyond his control.

She glanced down at her hand still on his. Eli had risked his life for her. Now, it was her turn to help him. No matter what it cost her, she would find out what really happened to Miriam. And then…

He'd been there in one of the best parts of her past. Would he have a place in her future?

The horse clomped through the wilderness with sure footing. Now that they'd put space between themselves and Vincent, she tried to relax, but it was hard because she knew Vincent wouldn't let a little blow to the head slow him down. He'd keep coming until she was dead, or he was in custody.

"Vincent's more afraid of the man he works for than he is of being arrested." Faith voiced her concerns aloud. "He has everything, including his life, to lose, if Ghost comes after him. And he will if Vincent doesn't handle the problem."

"We need to tell the sheriff what is happening, but with Vincent combing the community, I think it's best if we stay out of sight for a while."

Eli was right. Every minute they were out in the open they were in jeopardy. But Faith had to wonder if she would be putting her freedom at risk instead of Vincent if he actually followed through on his threat to frame her for Cheryl's death. It didn't matter. It was time to protect the ones she loved like she hadn't been able to protect Cheryl.

Eli skillfully maneuvered the buggy through the thin woods beyond the road. So far, there had been no sighting of Vincent through the gaps in foliage. Eli had been surprised he'd hit the man hard enough to knock him out. By now, he was convinced Vincent would be awake and searching for them. They couldn't slow down for a second.

"How did he get the second car?" Faith asked.

Only one explanation made sense.

"He probably stole it. Victoria was correct. He had some way of tracking the truck on his phone. I'm glad we were able to get it away from Aaron and Victoria's home, but I hope he didn't see their location before we moved it. I don't want that man near them."

The road to Aaron's homestead intersected the woods. Instead of getting on it, Eli turned the buggy right and ran parallel with the road.

"Do the rest of your brothers still live in West Koo-tenai?" Faith asked the question innocently enough. If only she'd realized the answer would be anything but.

While he struggled to respond, she turned toward him. Waited. Undoubtedly sensing something was off.

He did his best to answer without bringing up Mason. "Fletcher lives at our family homestead with *mamm*. Hunter has a place on the other side of the community." He stopped. Read the next question coming as if he had asked it himself.

"What about Mason? You two were always so close."

She was right. At one time, he and Mason had been close. They'd done everything together. Then, Mason, younger by a couple of years, became interested in Miriam without realizing she only had eyes for Eli.

When Mason first started talking about Miriam, Eli had wanted to tell his brother about the attraction he and Miriam shared, but Miriam had asked him to keep their courting secret until she spoke to her *daed*, so he had. Then Mason found out and became furious. Accused him of taking Miriam from him. Though Eli had tried to tell him the truth, Mason didn't want to hear it. The rift between the brothers grew. Mason left the faith before being baptized and moved away. A regret Eli carried with him to this day.

"He moved from the community many years ago."

Her brows rose. The questions were all there, yet she must have sensed he didn't want to talk about his *bruder* because she let it go.

The clearing near the family workshop came into view. Aaron and Fletcher created handcrafted furniture the family sold around the state. The sight of it was a relief. They were almost to Aaron's home.

"Your family still makes furniture?" Faith commented as they passed by the building.

"*Jah*. Aaron and Fletcher are the craftsmen of the

family. Hunter and I mill the lumber we harvest from the woods on our property."

Eli kept the gelding at a steady pace as they approached the house. He expelled a sigh of relief when he spotted the plume of woodstove smoke spiraling into the night air. The flicker of lantern light behind closed curtains. Each represented safety, but until they were inside, he wouldn't relax completely.

As the horse tramped along the path between the workshop and the house, a familiar yet disturbing sound traveled through his exhausted thoughts. A vehicle was heading down the road at a high rate of speed.

A second later, Faith heard it too. "Someone's coming." Her eyes latched on to his. "We'd better get out of sight while we still have time."

Eli commanded the gelding to a faster trot. Getting the buggy out of sight was critical. If this was Vincent, he'd seen them earlier. As a police officer, he was probably more observant than most and would likely recognize the buggy as theirs. Not many buggies would be out at this late hour. The last thing he wanted was to throw suspicion on the rest of the household if he hadn't already. His family had been through enough. They deserved better than for him to bring trouble to their doorstep, even though his *bruders* and *mamm* would tell him he was doing *Gott*'s will by helping those in need. And Faith was definitely in need.

When he reached the barn, Eli pulled up on the reins and climbed down. He didn't waste time getting the doors open while Faith drove the buggy inside.

Working together, they freed the horse, and Eli led the animal to its stall.

Outside, the wind howled around the corner of the

barn, carrying Eli's worst fear. The vehicle appeared to be heading toward Aaron's home.

Eli eased to the door and cracked it. Headlights bounced through the trees. He closed it and turned, almost slamming into Faith.

"Is it him?" Her panicked expression compelled him to ease her mind, but he couldn't because he believed it was Vincent. No one from the *Englisch* world would be visiting Aaron, especially at this time of the night.

NINE

"What do we do?" After their last run-in with Vincent, Faith couldn't imagine the level of his fury at having his plans foiled once again. The vehicle was almost right on top of them.

He looked her in the eyes. "We stay here."

Through the sliver of gaps in the walls, the headlights flashed across the barn. Faith ducked away from the wall as if Vincent could see her.

The vehicle rolled to a stop. A door slammed shut. Footfalls crunched along the gravel and up the steps.

Faith stood beside Eli and watched through the slats as a dark figure stood in the shadows of the porch and pounded on the door. Though their view was limited, the outline of Vincent's truck was visible.

The front door opened. Aaron stepped out onto the porch. From the lantern's glow, Vincent's angry profile was highlighted.

Faith grabbed on to Eli's arm for support. She couldn't make out what Vincent was saying but his stance was all threat.

He took a step closer to Aaron in recognizable intimidation. When Aaron didn't back down, Vincent shook his fist in his face.

"I'm asking you politely to leave my property," Faith heard Aaron say. Vincent appeared to hesitate.

"I'm going, but I know your brother is the one helping her… That's right. I know all about your brother and how he lives next to Faith's grandmother." Vincent's ominous laugh resounded among the silence. "If you're helping him, or her, you could get yourself into a lot of trouble. Maybe even end up dead." Vincent reached into his jacket pocket and Aaron stepped closer.

"I'm only showing you my badge, mister. I'll overlook the fact that you're taking a threatening stance with me for now, but I'm warning you. If you know where they're hiding, you'd better turn them over to me for your own good."

Aaron didn't waver. "I don't know anything about what you're talking about. You need to leave my property now."

"Fine," Vincent growled. "I'm leaving, but you should know when I come back, I will have the sheriff with me. He will force you to cooperate." With those angry words, he stormed to the truck and climbed inside. The engine fired and Vincent whipped around the vehicle and flew down the drive, spewing gravel everywhere.

And the words he'd spoken scared the daylights out of her.

"He's not telling the truth," Eli told her as if sensing the effects Vincent's lies had. "I don't believe he's ever spoken to the sheriff and he won't."

Faith turned to him. "I hope you're right, but I'm so scared, Eli."

Inches separated them. The strength she'd seen in him since childhood was still there. He would always be there for her.

"I won't let him hurt you. I promise," he whispered.

A breath slipped from her lips. Both moved. She went into his arms because it was as natural as breathing. He held her against his heart, and she was safe. All the fears that had followed her here, the ones that they both still faced, seeped from her body for just a little while.

She and Eli had history. Good history. But she also doubted. Not him—herself.

You felt the same way about Blake...

She'd believed everything Blake told her right from the beginning. He'd seemed like a true hero when she'd first met him in the ER after Blake had been shot while defending a fellow officer. She'd fallen hard, married quickly and spent ten years thinking she knew her husband.

But she'd been wrong. So wrong about Blake.

She pulled away and searched his eyes. More than anything, Faith wished she could believe what was happening between them now was more than a reaction to their desperate circumstances.

Eli didn't look away. "We should go inside. I'll feel safer there if he returns."

Her voice just wouldn't come out, so she nodded. Eli cracked the door and peeked outside before they left the confines of the barn.

Faith kept at his side as they crossed the yard to the porch.

Eli knocked several times. "It's me, Aaron." He wanted to make sure his brother knew Vincent hadn't returned.

Faith glanced around the darkness suppressing a shiver. Door locks slid open inside the house. Most who lived in this peaceful community rarely locked their doors. The fact that Aaron had chosen to spoke of how frightening Vincent's appearance here had been.

Aaron opened the door with a look of concern on his face. Eli ushered Faith inside and relocked the door.

"Are you both *oke*?" Aaron's frightened gaze shifted between them.

"We are." Eli explained what happened. "I'm sorry, *bruder*. I didn't mean to bring more troubles to your door."

"No, Eli, this is all my fault," Faith insisted. "I shouldn't have come back here."

Grandmother Sarah came over to where Faith stood beside Eli. "Nonsense, child. This was once your home. Where else would you go?"

She loved this woman so much, but her presence here in West Kootenai had endangered so many people already.

"Your *grossmammi* speaks the truth," Eli said. When she looked at him all she could think about was the tender moment they'd shared in the barn. "This man must be stopped before he kills you and anyone else he believes will stand in his way."

Vincent's threats had gone beyond just being directed at her. He intended to come after her grandmother and Eli. Now he'd threatened Aaron.

"The man who showed up on my porch tonight is capable of great violence," Aaron told her. "He will try to twist things to deceive people into believing he is a *gut*, law-abiding person."

"He's right, Faith," Victoria said. "You are doing the right thing and Sheriff Collins is an honorable man. He helped me. He will do the same for you."

Two weeks ago, when she'd found the evidence Blake left, she wasn't sure what to do with it. Faith had anguished over getting Cheryl involved. That decision had cost Cheryl her life. She couldn't afford to make any more wrong ones.

Eli understood how hard it was to let someone else in, but like him, Faith didn't have an option. He struggled to make the right decision under circumstances that were beyond his understanding. His gut told him they needed to get the sheriff involved as soon as possible, but he and Faith were both exhausted. They needed to take a breath to rest and gather their thoughts. Eli had no doubt Vincent would be trolling the community looking for them. They couldn't afford to make a mistake.

Help me, Gott. *I don't know what to do...*

"Supper is ready. Thanks to Sarah, I've mastered her friendship soup recipe." Victoria smiled at the older woman. "*Komm* and sit. We should enjoy the soup while it is still hot."

Eli glanced out the window, sure they were running out of time.

"It will be *oke* for a little while. You must eat, Eli," Victoria told him.

He waited while the family took their usual seats. Even though his *bruder* had welcomed him home, he was still getting used to being part of this loving family again.

Sarah clasped Faith's hand. Together they followed the family to the table where Faith stopped and looked back at him. There were questions in her eyes he couldn't answer. The tender moment they'd shared in the barn was unexpected, yet still burned in his thoughts.

Being close to her made him feel something he hadn't in a very long time, but he and Faith were wounded deeply. And the guilt he carried in his heart had become part of who he was just as assuredly as the heart that beat in his chest. Could he let it go? Believe himself deserving of this wonderful woman he cared so much about?

Eli claimed the seat beside Faith that Victoria indicated. A bowl of hearty friendship soup, brimming with split peas, lentils, barley, ground beef and tomatoes, was placed in front of him. The aroma reminded him of the hours that had passed since he'd eaten.

Once the table quieted, heads bowed. It was time for the silent prayer.

Eli lowered his head and closed his eyes. Though he knew *Gott* was always there, waiting for him to return, after what happened to Miriam, he'd struggled to find his way back to the Almighty.

Instead of praying, his thoughts wandered to the meals he'd shared with Miriam. Back then, everything seemed so perfect. Though what happened between him and *Bruder* Mason cut deeply, Miriam made him happy. They'd looked forward to a future with *kinner* of their own. And then everything was taken away.

"Amen," Aaron said aloud into the quiet room. The

lump in Eli's throat wouldn't go away. The past could not be changed. He'd hurt many people with his actions. Best to keep his head down and do his work. Not hope for anything more than what the Lord chose to give him.

"I will take my soup into the living room and keep watch in case Vincent shows up here." He carried the bowl from the room and resumed his earlier perch by the window.

As he dug into the soup with relish, all he could think about was getting to Eagle's Nest and speaking with the sheriff, but with Vincent out there somewhere, it was too risky for now.

"This is good." He turned at the sound of Faith's gentle voice. "I thought I would help you watch," she said.

He smiled at her consideration. *"Denki."*

"Your *mamm* always was a *gut* cook." Sarah brought her soup into the room to join them. She came over to Eli and patted his arm as if sensing the turmoil inside him.

"Things will work out in *Gott*'s timing," Sarah murmured as if she'd read his thoughts. She had a smile for him like so many times before. His old friend knew him well. She'd listened to him talk. Comforted him when he'd cried. Prayed for him when he didn't ask for it.

With his attention on the bowl in front of him, he didn't answer. Quiet conversation from the kitchen drifted their way. Growing up, he'd loved being from a big family. Meals, in particular, were a favorite. Now he was no longer sure of his place in the Shetler family.

"It's hard, isn't it?" Faith said with her attention on

his face. "Coming back to a past that was good and painful."

Despite his heavy heart, he smiled. "*Jah*, it is." She too had endured hardships in her life here in West Kootenai.

"It will get better." He wondered if she meant this for herself or for him. He hoped for both.

He nodded and spooned soup once more. For the first time since he'd returned, he didn't feel like he was standing on the outside looking into the life he wanted again.

When they'd finished their meal, Faith and Sarah carried the bowls to the kitchen.

Once Faith had helped with the cleanup, she returned to the living room and slipped into one of the rockers while Eli watched the darkness outside.

Time passed in silence as his worried thoughts went over everything they'd gone through. Did they risk leaving now when they had the cover of darkness working in their favor, or wait until morning and pray Vincent had left the immediate area? Frustration settled in. He had no idea.

With the fire dying in the woodstove, Eli added more wood. Once he was satisfied with the blaze, he sat beside Faith. The quiet between them wasn't awkward, which scared him. It reminded him of the many nights he and Miriam had shared like this. Once more, the past and all its failures returned to haunt him. Some men were better off alone.

While Eli pondered the future afforded to him, the smallest of sounds pulled his attention away. A board creaked near the door as if something or someone had stepped up on it. Footsteps paced across the porch. There would be no reason for anyone to be outside at this time of the evening. Which left only one explanation—Vincent was back.

TEN

Faith jumped to her feet. Before she could say a word, Eli held his finger to his lips and grabbed her hand, urging her toward the kitchen.

Aaron came forward as they approached. Eli stopped him before he spoke and moved close enough to whisper, "Someone's on the porch."

Aaron's eyes widened. Victoria hurried to her husband's side when she spotted his troubled expression.

"That man didn't go far," Aaron told her. "Faith, you and your *grossmammi* go upstairs with Eli and Caleb. Let Victoria and I handle this man. *Sohn*, show them where to go." The young man headed toward the stairs. Faith grabbed her grandmother's hand and followed with Eli.

"In here. This is my room," Caleb whispered and opened the closest door. They followed him inside. Caleb hurried to the window and looked out below to the porch. "I do not see anyone."

Eli cracked the door so they could hear. The front door opened. Boards squeaked.

"There's no one here," Aaron's deep voice said.

"But footprints are everywhere," Victoria insisted.

Faith bit her bottom lip. Someone had been out there minutes earlier. Where had Vincent gone?

The answer came quickly.

"What are you doing here?" Aaron again. This time tension filled his voice.

"You lied to me!" Vincent said. "I saw the buggy tracks leading onto the property. Your brother was here. Where are you hiding them?"

What sounded like a scuffle could be heard. Eli started out the door, but Faith grabbed his arm. "You can't go out there."

He turned toward her. The helpless look on his face pulled at her heart. She understood the guilt because she was drowning in it. This was her fault. If Aaron or Victoria were hurt, she would never be able to forgive herself.

"That's far enough." Victoria spoke up. "One more step and I will shoot. And I should warn you, I'm a former CIA agent. I don't miss."

An uncomfortable silence stretched out far too long.

"Alright, I'll leave. But I will find them wherever they're hiding. If you want to keep your brother out of jail—or worse, alive—I suggest you tell him to turn in the woman to me."

Faith's heart slammed against her chest. Seconds ticked by. The door finally closed. Aaron and Victoria waited until Vincent was gone before they came up the stairs and entered their son's room.

"You heard what was said?" Aaron asked.

Eli looked to Faith before answering. "*Jah*, we did. Do you think he left the property?"

"I can't be sure. He's incredibly determined." Victoria looked Faith's way. "A dirty cop with plenty to hide is a dangerous man. You are a major liability to him."

Faith blew out a breath. "I know and I'm so sorry I've brought this man to your home."

Victoria smiled. "There's nothing to be sorry for. I understand what it's like to be hunted by someone who wants you dead."

Faith admired this strong woman. "You were *Englisch* before you and Aaron married," she said, and Victoria nodded. Eli had told her little about the couple with the exception of Victoria not being from the community. She'd heard what the woman said. "You were once with the CIA?"

That someone from the CIA had chosen to leave the way of life behind and join the Amish community made her wonder if perhaps it wasn't too late for her. Maybe, even after being forced to leave her family behind, she could find her place here again.

She glanced at Eli, who watched their exchange with an unreadable expression on his face. Was he remembering the tragedy he'd faced with his wife? The suspicion he'd endured from law enforcement and his own community?

"I was born Amish, but my *mamm* died when I was five and I was forced to leave the only home I ever knew. I grew up *Englisch*. Joined the CIA and thought that was my place in life. But I never forgot my past and I spent most of my adult life trying to recapture the sense of community and the simple ways I loved so much as a child." She turned to her husband and smiled. "And then I came here and met Aaron. He helped me find my way back."

It sounded so simple, but until Vincent's threat was

eliminated, she couldn't think about a future here among the Plain people she'd once called family.

"It wasn't easy for me either," Victoria said, interrupting her concerns. "I had people coming after me who wanted me dead. But with Aaron and some *gut* people, including Sheriff Collins from Eagle's Nest, I was able to free myself of the past and let go of that life. You can too. With Sheriff Collins's help, I will use my former connections to help bring down Vincent and the rest of his corrupt cops."

Faith prayed her story would have the happy ending Victoria's did. "Thank you," she said with a sigh.

"You and Sarah are part of our family now," Victoria assured her. "And your family will help you through this. So, why don't you start from the beginning and tell me everything you know about this man. Let me see what I can do to get the ball rolling in a new direction."

Even though Faith was a long way from being free of Vincent, the weight of the past few days slowly lifted. She wasn't alone. She had her grandmother and these wonderful people. And she had Eli. More than anything, she wanted to walk past this valley of death and step toward being happy again. Was it possible? Only *Gott* knew.

"She is a *gut* woman. It's a shame she's caught up in something like this," Aaron said when it was just the two of them. He added more wood to the stove before looking to Eli. "I remember little Faith from when her *mamm* and *daed* lived here."

Eli watched his *bruder* stir the fire and realized there was more coming.

"You always had a soft spot for Faith, and you've been alone for several years."

Eli couldn't let him finish. "I am only helping her because of Sarah. She is worried about her grand-daughter. And as you said, Faith and I were once close." Aaron watched him without saying a word. Eli felt the need to add, "She has no one to look out for her. That's not right."

Aaron clasped Eli's shoulder. "I am not telling you how to live your life, *bruder.* I know how much you loved Miriam, but she's gone, and she wouldn't want you to mourn forever. You deserve to be happy. To be a *daed.* Have a family of your own. *Kinner* around your table."

Each word struck deep in his heart. "I am a *daed*—or I was to be. Miriam was pregnant when she died." The only person he'd told about the baby before now was Faith.

The surprise on Aaron's face turned to pity. "I'm so sorry, Eli. I didn't know."

Eli fought against the hurt that was always there. "How can I simply move on with my life when they are gone because of me."

"The fire was not your fault. You deserve happiness, Eli. It's time you believed that for yourself."

Before Eli could respond, Faith came into the room. Her distraction was a welcome one. Helping her eased his conscience a little. Maybe that was why *Gott* brought him back to West Kootenai? To help her. Sarah. He would seek ways to fulfill his Godly purpose and not expect anything more.

"Do you think he's still out there?" she asked, as if seeking his reassurance.

Eli came over to where she stood. "I doubt it, but I will have a look around outside to ease your mind. You should try to get some rest."

She ran her hand across her eyes. "Thank you, but I can't sleep knowing he's still out there. I'm coming with you."

Exposing her to another one of Vincent's attacks was something he wanted to avoid. "It would be safer for you to remain here." Eli turned to his older *bruder* for support, but she wasn't having it.

"I'll be okay, and I have to do something." She threw up her hands. "I can't sit around and wait for Vincent's next attack to happen."

Aaron grabbed his shotgun from near the door where Eli had placed it earlier. "Victoria and I will come with you. It will be safer with more people." Aaron turned to his *fraa*.

The love between Aaron and Victoria was clear in the way they looked at each other…and it gave him hope that perhaps one day he would be free of the guilt he carried on his shoulders, because he was so weary of it.

"I don't think we can risk using any lights," Eli said. The last thing they needed was something to direct Vincent to their location.

Aaron and Victoria slipped outside and waited while Faith and Eli did the same.

"Victoria and I will head toward the workshop," Aaron told them. "Be careful."

"We will." He watched Aaron and his wife start for the workshop before he faced Faith. "Stay close to me." The chill bouncing between his shoulder blades warned him they might be walking into a trap Vincent set.

With her at his side, he crossed the yard to the barn. Instead of using the main entrance, he slipped through the side door with Faith.

There were no signs Vincent had been there. Eli wasn't sure what he'd hoped for. Another run-in certainly wasn't it, but he did want this to be over for Faith.

He reached for her hand and held it. The uneasy feeling continued to grow.

"He's not been here," he said. "Perhaps he figured we kept going and he's moved on. We should go back to the house. As soon as it's light out, we'll head to phone shanty and call the sheriff. We need his help to bring down Vincent. I just hope he isn't expecting that move."

She kept her attention on his face. "Whatever happens, Eli, I want you to know how much I appreciate you risking your life for me."

He looked at her and saw things he never thought possible again. A future. A *fraa. Kinner.*

But how could two damaged people hope to have any of those things?

With Gott, all things were possible…the thought was placed in his mind as if from above.

"*Komm*, let's head back to the others." He started for the door again when a noise outside stopped him in his tracks. Someone was moving around near the back of the barn. It couldn't be Aaron and Victoria. They were searching near the workshop so far away. But if it wasn't them, then… Vincent.

Eli grabbed Faith's hand and tugged her along beside him until they were hidden in one of the empty stalls.

The door opened. Someone stepped inside the barn. Had Vincent seen them come inside?

Please, Gott, no.

It was up to him alone to keep Faith safe.

A cell phone shrilled, echoing through the cavernous space. Eli's heart almost jumped out of his chest when he realized the man stopped next to where they hid.

"Hello." Vincent's tone was laced with anger as he answered the call. Eli hoped the call would distract him and he wouldn't search the stalls.

"Yes, sir." In an instant, Vincent changed his tune. "Yes, I do know where she is, and I will take care of her soon. Don't worry, I have this under control. I will call you once it's finished."

Who was this person Vincent spoke to?

"No, there's no need to come here. As I've said, I have it under control. She's not walking out of here alive." Silence followed and Eli could just make out Vincent's astonished expression through the slats in the stall door. His brow was furrowed as he listened. "Five hours! That's not much time... No, I can handle it. And if she told anyone else about what Blake wrote, I'll take care of them, as well."

A moment of silence followed before Vincent expelled a menacing sigh and slapped the nearby shovel across the barn. The gelding whinnied along with the cow, but Vincent paid no mind. The side door slammed against the wall. Vincent stormed from the building.

Eli was too shocked to move for the longest time. He and Faith huddled in the empty stall while he prayed the man would leave the property for good, but Eli feared Vincent would search every square inch of the place.

After what felt like an eternity, they slipped from their hiding spot.

"I can't believe that just happened," she murmured, in as much shock as he was.

"Who do you think he was speaking with?"

She looked him in the eye. "My guess would be the drug dealer he works for. Ghost. And if that's the case, then this is bad. Really bad. If Ghost comes here, he'll bring an army."

ELEVEN

"The enclosed buggy should keep us mostly hidden from view," Eli said to ease her fears. She appreciated his efforts. But until Vincent was in jail, she couldn't let down her guard for a second because she wasn't sure how many more run-ins with him they would survive. "If we take the back way into the community, we may have a chance at using the phone without Vincent spotting us. I'll feel better once we are able to tell Sheriff Collins what's been happening."

Faith watched the woods pass by while the conversation she and Eli had overheard the night before replayed in her head. More than the five-hour deadline had passed. Vincent's employer had given him an ultimatum. Find her, or he'd take over the search. When he did, he wouldn't need Vincent any longer.

"Do you think he'll really come here?" she asked. Faith couldn't imagine how bad things would become if a ruthless drug dealer showed up in this peaceful community.

"I sure hope not." He shook his head, exhaustion clinging to him. He'd survived a gunshot and countless attacks from a man determined to end their lives, and they were still no closer to being free of Vincent's threat. "Once we speak to the sheriff, and perhaps get Victoria involved, I'll feel better."

She smiled despite the circumstances. "I will too."

Only *Gott* knew what their outcome would be, but she had to believe He wouldn't want her or Eli to pay the price for Vincent's crimes.

The horse clomped along the path leading to the road and Faith's mind returned to the years she'd spent here in West Kootenai. The times she and Eli had been together were some of the best.

"Do you miss this way of life?" Eli asked almost as if she'd spoken her thoughts aloud.

"I guess I do. For so long, I've wanted to come back, but the thought of returning to the community without my grandparents was just too hard."

"You are home now," Eli said. "And regrets won't change anything."

Home. The word hadn't felt the same since she left West Kootenai. No matter where she lived, this would always be home.

Something changed in his eyes when he glanced her way. She bit her bottom lip and gazed into his eyes wanting so much. Eli leaned closer. She touched his face. Read the uncertainty in his eyes. Eli was nothing like Blake, and for that she was glad. The gentleness she found in this rock of a man shattered all her doubts and made her want to keep fighting. Hoping. Praying there was a chance for them.

The mare snorted and the tender moment passed. Her hand dropped away and she struggled to recapture her composure.

Eli blew out a breath and faced forward.

Did he feel the connection between them changing? Or was he remembering the woman he'd lost? The love they shared that could never be replaced. The promise of a family gone.

Once, she and Blake had talked about starting a family, but there never seemed to be the right time. She'd wanted a baby for so long. She'd cried over the lost opportunity when Blake passed away and thought she'd spend the rest of her life grieving. Then, she'd found his note and the pain of losing him was over-shadowed by the crimes he'd committed.

She was in the middle of a fight for her life. The future and its possibilities were something she didn't have the luxury of thinking about right now. If she wanted to live long enough to bring Cheryl and Blake's killer to justice, she had to keep her head on straight and not get bogged down by what-ifs.

The community shops appeared through the trees in front of them. Though darkness still clung to most of the countryside, the owners of the Amish businesses were hard at work. The café where Eli enjoyed a meal on occasion was open for service. The Grabers served the best *frühstück* around, and the Amish bakery fry pies were famous in the community.

Eli guided the mare along the slushy path. Last evening was the first night that it hadn't snowed since he'd been home. The clear skies were a welcomed relief.

He caught glimpses of several buggies along with a few cars parked in front of the café. Many of the *Englischers* around the area came to the community to enjoy the Grabers's cooking.

The buggy slowly eased past the back of the café and

the bulk-food store. One of the last shops at the end of the businesses was the bakery. The Stoltzfuses were *gut* people who had an additional bakery in Eagle's Nest. Their *dochder* and her *mann* had taken over the running of the original bakery here in West Kootenai.

"Those cinnamon rolls smell so good," Faith said with a hint of wistfulness that was hard to resist. Though it was best if they kept moving, if they pulled the buggy around back, what would it hurt to purchase a couple of fresh-baked cinnamon rolls to go?

Eli headed the buggy toward the back of the building and out of sight. Faith turned to him with raised brows.

"We will only stop for a second."

She smiled. "Thank you."

He stepped from the buggy and held out his hand. More and more, his heart was opening up to Faith. His feelings growing. They shared history and he wanted to make her happy.

Eli knocked on the back door and Sadie Zook peeked out the window, smiled and unlocked the door.

"*Gut* morning, Eli." Sadie's gaze shifted to Faith and Eli introduced her.

"We're here for two of your cinnamon rolls to go."

Sadie nodded and stepped behind the counter. "Daniel just put out a fresh batch." She removed two of the largest rolls and placed them in a bag. "Would you like *kaffe* to go along with them?"

Eli looked to Faith, who nodded. "*Jah*, two for the road."

While Sadie filled their order, Eli glanced out the window at the burgeoning new day. The street in front of the bakery was illuminated by headlights. Someone coming to enjoy a warm breakfast, perhaps. The knot in Eli's stomach had him on edge.

He grabbed Faith's arm and pulled her along beside him until they reached the kitchen and were away from the view of the windows.

Sadie's husband, Daniel, appeared surprised by their sudden arrival in his kitchen.

Eli did his best to explain. "Someone bad is looking for Faith. We have to stay out of sight here, please."

"Who is after you?" Daniel asked, his expression growing troubled.

"An *Englischer* from New York. He's trying to kill me," Faith told him. "He's driving a dark-colored truck."

The shock on Daniel's face was clear, but he did not hesitate. "I've seen this truck around the community. He stopped in here and was asking questions about you, but I had no idea what he was talking about," he told Faith.

Sadie came into the room. "What is going on?"

After Eli explained, Sadie's eyes widened. She glanced back to the dining area. "I saw him pass by, as well. I thought it curious because he's an *Englischer* and he's been hanging around the community."

Vincent had been combing the community for them two days. "He's up to no good," Eli said. "Did you see which way he went?"

Sadie nodded. "*Jah*, he is heading back toward your family's property."

The news was unsettling. Was Vincent going back to Aaron's home? Eli was grateful his *bruder* had thought ahead and taken the family to *Mamm*'s house, but what would happen when Vincent realized the family was gone? By now, he'd know Eli's *mamm* lived close by.

"Stay here," Daniel told them. "I will check for his truck."

The three waited in the kitchen while Daniel stepped outside. He was only gone a few minutes before he returned.

"There's no sign of him. He must have kept going."

"*Denki*, Daniel. We should be on our way before he returns." Eli hesitated. "I hate to ask this of you, but I'm worried about Sarah's animals and mine. We had to leave them behind. Could you please stop by our places to make sure they are cared for? And my mare was set loose by the creek. I'd appreciate it if you'd confirm she made it home."

Daniel nodded. "*Jah*, I'll take care of it."

"*Denki.* Please be careful." Eli paid for the sweets, then he and Faith headed out the back entrance.

Once they were safely ensconced in the buggy again, Eli directed the mare back onto the road.

Faith handed him a coffee and cinnamon roll. He accepted it, but his appetite for the sweet was gone. All he could think about was his family's safety.

His thoughts returned to the conversation they'd overheard the night before. Vincent was involved with a dangerous person. He stood to lose much if the information Faith had on him went public. And there was no doubt Vincent knew this. He was all out of time to contain the problem before the thug from New York did it for him. Ghost wouldn't want to leave any witnesses behind, which meant Vincent was in serious danger of losing his life.

They reached Eli's family's furniture shop, where

some of the pieces Aaron and Fletcher made were sold. As they started past it toward the community phone shanty, Eli's heart sank. Vincent's truck was parked behind the building out of sight. Somehow, the man must have circled back around without them seeing it.

"Oh, no." Faith spotted the vehicle at the same time he did.

Eli's mind raced with decisions. Turning back wasn't an option at this point. It would call more attention. "Quick. Get in the back and out of sight," he told her while he kept his attention on the truck.

So far, Vincent hadn't looked up. He appeared to be studying something in his hand.

Faith clambered over the bench seat to the two seats in the back that faced each other.

Once she was in place, he felt somewhat better prepared. Eli clamped the hat down as low as it could get it and still see where he was going. With his heart pounding, he passed by the parked truck. Vincent glanced up at that moment and looked straight at him.

Eli prayed he hadn't left a lasting impression on the dirty cop. Because if he had, Vincent wouldn't waste time coming after them.

TWELVE

Faith crouched out of sight and tried to keep from panicking. This was a different buggy than they'd used before. Vincent would have no way of knowing it was them unless he got a good look at Eli.

"We're past him," Eli murmured while keeping a close watch behind them.

"Did he recognize you?" Faith asked from her crouched position.

"I'm not sure. He looked right at me. But I can't be certain."

Faith peeked out the back window and watched the truck slowly ease from the road. Was Vincent simply tired of sitting still and had decided to search someplace else or…

"He's pulling onto the road," she said, and Eli whirled around in his seat. There was no doubt. Vincent was coming their way.

Eli picked up the mare's speed, but the truck continued to gain on them until he was within a few feet of the buggy. The noise of the powerful engine spooked the mare, who slung around her head and side-stepped down the road.

While Eli tried to calm the horse, Vincent plowed into the back of the buggy, sending it lurching forward. The mare whinnied and reared up on her hind legs.

Vincent revved up behind them again and prepared for another attack.

"If he hits us again, the buggy will splinter apart," Eli said in a tight voice. "Come up here and take the reins. Keep the mare as steady as you can."

Faith quickly scrambled over the seat. Eli handed her the controls and grabbed the shotgun. Faith's heart threatened to explode in her chest as she gripped them tightly and kept her attention on the mare who wanted to flee the danger behind them. While she struggled to hold on to the animal, Eli leaned out of the buggy and fired.

Faith glanced over her shoulder in time to see the truck veer off the road and come to a jarring stop in the foot-deep ditch that was covered in snow.

"We have to get off this road before he comes after us again," Eli said in a strained tone. And she had no doubt Vincent would.

In front of them, the Lake Koocanusa bridge came into view. Crossing the bridge was far too dangerous. If Vincent caught up with them there, he'd push them over the side, and no one would ever be the wiser.

"There's an old logging trail off to the right. It's rarely used anymore, but we don't have a choice." Eli leaned forward and watched for the road.

Faith kept a careful eye on Vincent. Dark smoke shot from the tailpipes as he got the truck running again. He didn't waste time getting back on the road.

"He's coming," Faith warned.

"There's the trail. It's pretty overgrown, so I'm hoping he won't be able to fit the truck inside." Eli coaxed the mare onto what could barely be called a trail. The path was just wide enough for the buggy to fit through. Trees that hadn't been pruned in years scraped along the sides.

The horse was still on edge from what happened and continued to sling her head around in a fretful motion.

A tree limb grated along the side of the buggy, probably taking paint along with it.

"After what's happened, I don't think it's wise to use the phone. Vincent will probably be expecting that move. We need to get the buggy and ourselves out of sight as quickly as possible because he knows what we're driving, and he'll be looking for us."

While she understood they couldn't afford to stay in plain sight, the thought of retreating stung of failure.

Eli kept the mare at a fast clip despite the cramped conditions.

She looked behind them and could no longer see the road. "I sure hope he doesn't try to follow us."

Eli held her gaze. "He's determined."

His words didn't settle the nerves in the pit of her stomach.

Eli entwined their fingers. "I don't believe he can fit that big truck through the opening, but he definitely saw which way we went, and he'll be looking for another way to cut us off. He'll expect us to return to Aaron's place. If he goes there, he'll find it empty."

But he'd keep looking for them. Vincent would check every place where they'd been until he found them.

"We need to find a safe place to hide until he has

moved from the area." But it had been years since she'd last visited the community. She was all turned around.

"There's an old logging camp close by. It's pretty much been reclaimed by the woods. I don't see how Vincent could find us there."

They were safe for now, but how long would it last?

It had been years since Eli visited the logging camp. As boys, he and his *bruders* used to explore every square inch of the woods around the community. Once they were older, they'd hunted for food near here.

He stopped the buggy, and they both got out. The damage from the tree branches was great. There were deep grooves on both sides.

"It can be fixed," Eli assured her, but she shook her head and turned away.

He clasped her arms and turned her to face him, spotting the tears in her eyes. "It can be fixed, and this isn't your fault."

"I set this in motion," she murmured in a shaky voice. "All of it."

Eli gathered her in his arms. "I wish I could erase him from your life so you wouldn't have to go through any of this, but I can't. So, I will do the next best thing and be by your side until Vincent is in jail."

Holding her close, it scared him how much he felt she belonged there.

She pulled away and smiled up at him. Tears dampened her cheeks, and he brushed his thumb across them. More than anything he wanted to kiss her. Hold her close. Wish away the danger coming after them. But he couldn't and he needed to stay focused.

He let her go and stepped away. "Let's keep going,"

he said. "If I remember correctly, the camp should be right through there."

Thick overgrowth would make it impossible to get the buggy through. "Let's see if we can reach the camp first, then we'll find another way to bring in the buggy." He glanced at the mare with doubts. "I don't like leaving her here alone for long, especially when she's so spooked."

Eli thought about his mare that Vincent had deliberately let loose. Had the animal made it home safely? Once he was able, he'd return and make sure the horse was there.

He did his best to calm the worried animal while Faith watched the path.

Once the mare had been quieted, he tied the reins to a tree.

Eli read every single one of Faith's misgivings. "We'll be fine. Stay close to me, *oke*?" He stepped into the thicket with her behind him.

"How do you know about this logging camp?" she asked. "Did you work here before?"

He smiled to himself at her assumption. "*Nay*. It was shut down long before I was old enough to work as a logger. My *bruders* and I used to explore the area."

Working their way through the thick brush was challenging. Perspiration formed on his brow despite the cool weather.

"You and your brothers always did fun things together. I loved it when you let me tag along."

Eli remembered the sweet little girl who wanted to be part of everything they did. "And it almost got you into trouble a couple of times."

One incident in particular came to mind. It was one

of those times when she'd followed Eli and his *bruders* into the woods. "Like the time you decided to pick some wild blueberries." Eli had noticed her wandering off and followed. "That black bear wasn't happy with you trying to poach his food."

"Oh, I remember that day." Faith started laughing. "I thought you were mad at me."

"Not mad, only worried," he corrected. "You always were a curious child, and your *grossdaddi* encouraged your adventurous spirit."

The woods in front of them began to thin. "This is it." They'd reached the camp, and no sign of Vincent met them.

Eli stepped into the clearing and glanced around. The woods were slowly reclaiming most of the buildings. Rusted equipment was sinking into the earth.

On the opposite side of the camp, a trail appeared usable. Though he had no doubt the place hadn't been operational in years, someone from the community visited frequent enough to leave a trail. Eli hoped Vincent wouldn't stumble onto it.

"We can bring the mare in through there." He pointed to the spot. Together they fought their way back to the buggy and eased it forward until Eli picked up the trail leading into the camp.

Once they were back in camp, Eli led the mare behind the one building that appeared to still be useable. He tied the animal to a nearby tree and out of the wind before he returned with the bucket of oats he'd brought for the trip. She'd need water, but he'd search for that once she'd finished her meal.

"Shall we see if we can get out of the cold for a bit?" He glanced up at the clear sky. The sun was shining, yet the temperature was closing in on freezing. Life in the mountains.

Faith tugged her jacket tighter and agreed. "That's a good idea. It's cold out."

He went over to the front of the building and twisted the knob. While it moved, the door didn't. The frame was swollen shut by years of snow and rain.

Putting his full weight into it, Eli tried again. It gave a little. Two more tries and they were inside.

The place was set up to be barracks for those working in the camp. It was basic and typical of most logging camps—a couple of chairs, several cots spread around the room and a potbellied stove in the center to warm the entire space.

Though a fire would take away the chill, it was too risky. Vincent might spot the smoke.

"At least it's warmer than outside in the wind," he said and looked at the exhaustion that clung to Faith's face.

"This must be a primitive way to live." She glanced around the dust-covered space.

"It is." He recalled his time in the logging camp near Libby. "It's a place to eat and sleep. Nothing more."

She peered out one of the grimy windows. "How long do you think we should wait here before we can leave?"

Eli had no idea what Vincent could be thinking. "I'm not sure. A while. I'm hoping he'll think we worked our way out of the woods and returned to my house."

"Which means we can't go back there or to my grandmother's place."

He agreed. "It will be too dangerous. The same goes for Aaron's place, but we'll need my *bruder*'s help.

Using the phone near the community businesses is too risky with Vincent hanging around. He may be watching the phone shanty now, expecting us to reach out for help. I'll ask Fletcher to head to the sheriff's station in Eagle's Nest and tell him what's been happening. So far, Vincent hasn't seen his face. Hopefully, the sheriff will be able to come to us."

It wasn't much of a plan, but it was the best he could think of on short notice and he felt better having it. For now, they just had to stay out of sight.

Faith came over to where he stood and cupped his cheek with a tender look on her face. "You've never doubted my innocence, which couldn't have been easy."

His protective instincts resurfaced as he stared into her beautiful eyes. He deeply cared for her. She'd always been important to him, even as a child, but he wasn't worthy of her. He'd let down Miriam. He wouldn't do that to Faith.

Eli stepped back and turned away, his heart heavy. He had nothing to offer her but trouble. And she had enough of that on her own.

THIRTEEN

It was frightening how quickly life changed. A year ago, hers appeared perfect on the surface. A handsome husband. A great career that she loved. And then...

The foundation holding her world together crumbled and she realized everything had been a lie. There was nothing perfect about her life.

Her attention came back to Eli. Childhood memories returned. Her hand in his as they walked the path to her house. If she closed her eyes, she could almost feel the rough callouses on his hand from hard work. The ready smile that was always close whenever she said something funny or if he decided to tease her. It was as if he'd been imprinted on her heart for years, waiting for this time. Their time?

Something must have showed on her face because Eli came over to where she stood.

"Is something wrong?" He'd misunderstood the sudden heat in her cheeks. The quick pulse that she was sure he'd heard.

Faith cleared her throat. "No, I was just remembering how you used to tease me when we were little."

His lips lifted into a smile. "That's because you were easy to tease. You took everything so seriously."

Her eyes widened. This unburdened side of him mesmerized her. "Of course, I was." She pretended to be offended but her smile gave it away. This was the Eli she'd grown up knowing. Before the cares of the world weighted him down, much as they had her. If only they both could go back to that simple time.

"I loved everything about this life back then. My grandfather was my hero. He taught me so many things and we'd have these wonderful adventures together."

"Oh, I remember. Like the time your *grossdaddi* told you lost treasure was hidden in the woods and you both went in search of it." A glint of mischief hinted in Eli's eyes.

"Are you saying buried treasure isn't really in the woods?" Faith held a straight face as long as she could before she burst out laughing. "I'm only kidding. I know he was only pretending for me and I loved him for it."

Eli chuckled along with her. "He was. I miss your *grossdaddi* and mine. Those two were so much fun together. They grew up here. Never thought about leaving West Kootenai. They loved the land. Their families. The Plain way of life that focused on *Gott* and family above all else."

She swallowed several times. "It's a special way of life most people never fully understand."

He didn't respond, but his dark eyes watched her in a way that made her yearn for the impossible.

"I really miss this life," she said with a catch in her voice. "I wish…"

His eyes held hers captive. "What do you wish?"

She shook her head. "That I'd never left West Kootenai. I wish my father hadn't dragged us away from everyone we loved. And I wish that I'd never met Blake St. Clair." Her voice died into a sob and he tugged her close.

Crying was a weakness she couldn't afford, yet the regrets she had brought tears to the surface. Coming on the heels of a year of grief, discovering the truth about Blake's crimes had destroyed any good memories she had of her marriage.

"Things happen for a purpose. Even the bad things." A touch of regret hung in his voice and she pulled a little away.

He'd been through so much himself. Losing his wife and child in such a violent way had to have been horrific. Then being accused of causing their deaths.

She brushed her palm across his cheek. "I'm so sorry. I know how much you loved Miriam."

He looked into her eyes and clasped her hand. "I did. I thought I'd died with her and the *kinna*."

A love like that didn't come along but once in a lifetime. She thought she'd had it with Blake.

"But *Gott* had different plans for me. He wanted me to go on." He shook his head. "So, I do. I get up each day and I work hard and try to understand His purpose."

Tears filled her eyes. She hated to admit it but she was jealous of the relationship Eli had shared with Miriam.

He spotted the tears and brushed a calloused thumb across them, a look of wonder on his face. "Why are you crying?"

How did she put into words the depth of sorrow in

her heart? "I always thought Blake and I had a fairy-tale marriage. That nothing could pull us apart, but to be honest with you, for a few years before his death, we'd been drifting apart. We rarely spent time together. He worked long hours and when he wasn't working, he barricaded himself in his office for hours at a time. He kept so many things secret from me."

As she looked into his handsome face, something inside her stilled. She waited for him. He leaned down and touched his lips to hers. The gentleness was her undoing. A dying sob escaped, and she kissed him back, her hands framing his face. She'd forgotten how much she once cared for Eli. Looked up to him. Had a crush on him. At one time wanted to grow up and marry him.

The kiss ended so abruptly that it took a second for her catch up. Eli was inches away, but he wasn't looking at her, but the window. His head cocked to one side.

"Did you hear that?" he asked.

The tender moment between them evaporated when she did. Someone was tromping through the underbrush and heading straight for the camp.

Eli quickly covered the space to the grimy window hidden beneath dust-covered tattered curtains. He edged them apart while Faith peered over his shoulder.

Vincent emerged on the opposite side of the camp. Eli let the curtain drop and went over to the front door and clicked the lock. It would amount to little if Vincent tried to get inside but gave Eli a sense of slightly more control.

"We can't stay here," Faith told him. "He'll search every building in the camp."

And they couldn't leave by the way they'd come. Which left the back door.

"Keep an eye on him and I'll see if I can open the door without making too much noise. If he starts this way, let me know." Eli tried the doorknob. It proved as difficult to open as the front.

"He's checking on the opposite side of the camp, but most of those quarters are falling apart. It won't be long before he tries this one."

Eli freed the door. "Hurry, Faith." He grabbed her hand and started outside. "We'll have to get to the buggy and hope we can get a head start before he hears us." Vincent would be armed and ready to shoot them on sight.

The mare saw them approaching and dipped back her ears. Eli reached her side and did his best to soothe the animal before she made a sound.

"Get inside and stay out of sight," he whispered. "I'll lead the mare through the woods until we're away from the camp. With me close, I hope she'll remain quiet."

"Be careful," she whispered, her eyes frozen wide and fearful.

He waited until she was safe before he grabbed the mare's bridle and started walking toward the treed area behind the barracks. Though he did his best to be quiet, it was impossible to move a buggy and mare sound-lessly over frozen ground.

Once they reached the last building in the camp, Eli eased down the buggy's side and peered around. Vincent stood in the middle of the camp looking in their direction.

Eli ran back to the buggy and climbed inside. "He heard us," he told Faith. The mare bolted toward the trail opening someone had carved from the woods, as if sensing danger. Eli gripped the leather straps tight in a desperate attempt to contain the spooked animal but finally loosened his hold and let the mare charge toward freedom.

A glance behind them proved Vincent wasn't giving up even on foot. "Stay down," Eli warned when he spotted the weapon in Vincent's hand. Seconds later, the back of the buggy was riddled with bullets. Eli did his best to remain out of sight and still see what he was doing.

The mare ran harder, her mane fanning upward in the wind she created. Froth flew from her mouth.

"Where did he leave his truck?" Faith asked the question Eli hadn't had time to consider.

"He must have left it out on the road and walked in." The overgrowth thinned as the road appeared in front of them. Eli pulled hard on the reins to get the horse to slow to a fast trot.

On the side near the woods, Vincent had left his truck. An idea occurred that might buy them time enough to escape. Eli brought out the shotgun. "Come up here. I'm going to try something," he told her as she scrambled to the seat beside him.

He gave her the reins and opened the door. "I'm going to shoot out his tires."

While Faith kept the animal under control, Eli leaned out and fired at one of the front tires. It blew on impact. He reloaded and shot the second one out.

That should keep Vincent from following. He closed the door and set the shotgun at his feet.

Faith handed him back the reins and glanced over her shoulder. "He's almost to the road."

Eli whipped around in time to see Vincent emerge from the woods and empty his weapon in their direction. Several shots damaged the back of the buggy before the vehicle was no longer in range. For the moment, they were safe.

A thankful prayer slipped through his head. "That was scary."

"Yes, it was." She held out her hands. "I'm shaking all over. How long before he finds another way to come after us?"

Eli looked her in the eye. "He managed to get a car before. He'll find a way to get another vehicle."

"This just keeps getting worse," she said and rubbed her temples. "What are we going to do?"

"We go to *Mamm*'s house and Fletcher can fetch the sheriff right away." Eli hoped he sounded more confident than he felt.

A pronounced sigh slipped from her lips. "I have a feeling it's only a matter of time before the person Vincent spoke to last night arrives here."

If that happened the community would be caught in the middle of an all-out war between two dangerous men, and he and Faith would be completely outnumbered. The sheriff had to be warned about the upcoming battle. Because anyone who got in their way would be fair game. Including the Eagle's Nest Sheriff's department. Including Eli and Faith.

FOURTEEN

An exhaustion that went beyond physical burrowed down deep. Just when Faith thought it couldn't get any worse, it did.

She'd brought shame to her family and harm to everyone around her. Now an all-out invasion was coming to this peaceful community. All because of her selfishness.

As the buggy continued down the road, Eli slowed the horse to a trot and directed her onto a smaller dirt road. He was doing his best to keep them out of harm's way. Faith was grateful he was thinking for them both because she couldn't sling a single coherent thought together.

Time stretched out filled with its own fears. Her mind continued replaying the terrible things that had happened since she'd arrived in West Kootenai.

"Do you remember that one time our families went down to the creek for a picnic?" Eli said.

She twisted toward him and tried to recall the time he spoke of. "I don't… Oh wait, I do," she said, and started laughing. It had been a warm summer day for Montana. Both families had gotten into the routine of sharing a picnic several times during the warm months. They'd go to Silver Creek, two wagons filled to the brim with their members and food.

"That day was perfect," she said, but he gave her strange look.

"What day are you remembering?" He cocked his head toward her with a grin on his face.

Her eyes widened, but then she recalled and shook her head.

The women in the families had prepared their best dishes. Eli and his brothers had put together two picnic tables to make room for everyone to be seated.

Grandmother Sarah had purchased two exceptionally large watermelons as a treat because they were not always available so far north.

When no one was looking, the Shetler brothers snuck away with one of the melons. They'd planned to split it among themselves. Unsurprisingly, Mason was the ringleader of the caper.

Only the boys' grandfather had spotted them and gone to investigate. At the time, he hadn't realized Faith had followed him.

The boys had the knife ready and were just about to start cutting when Levi confronted them. Mason tossed the melon to Aaron, who passed it to Fletcher and on along to Hunter. Hunter got nervous and he meant to chuck it to Eli, but instead it landed at Levi's feet. The melon burst into pieces. Juice went flying all over Levi, and Eli started laughing and couldn't stop.

Faith had been so sure everyone involved would get in serious trouble.

Levi Shetler had glanced from the broken melon to the boys and burst out laughing himself. Then, he reached down and tossed pieces of the watermelon at each of the boys. Soon, an all-out food fight began, and Faith was right in the middle of it. By the end, everyone was covered in sticky watermelon juice, including Faith. They'd waded out into the creek and washed off as best they could.

"I remember Grandmother Sarah's expression when we all showed up at the table soaking wet." It had been a huge joke for weeks following.

"I was so sure *Grossdaddi* was going to kill us all," Eli said with a chuckle.

She grinned at him. Eli was trying to distract her from the troubles they faced and for that she was grateful. "I thought so too. But he was always an easygoing man. And he loved you boys so much."

Eli nodded. "*Jah*, he did. He taught me about logging and about life. He sent me a letter after Miriam and I moved to Libby. *Grossdaddi* always tried to talk me into returning. He said it would all work out with Mason in time, but it didn't." His jaw flexed and he looked over at her. "I guess we both have parts of our past we wish we could change."

"I guess we do."

Looking back at the time, the little girl she'd been couldn't have imagined that way of life ending, but it did. By summer's end, her family had packed up and called an Amish taxi to take them to Billings. From there, they'd taken a bus far away to strange places she never imagined. Big cities with different ways of life. And she'd hated it.

A thousand times over she'd wished she'd returned to West Kootenai when she was old enough. Come home where she belonged and had those precious years with her *grossdaddi*.

She couldn't change the past, but she could do everything in her power to make sure she never left the community or her grandmother again.

No matter what the future held for her and Eli, if they survived Vincent's rampage, she was home. Finally, back where she belonged.

Eli kept away from the shops this time as a precaution. Glimpses of them peeked through the trees. The path they were on ran parallel to the main road. Though he'd incapacitated Vincent's truck, Eli couldn't let down his guard. These past few days had left them with no time to catch their breaths in between Vincent's attacks. He was worn out to the bone. He couldn't imagine how tired Faith must be.

She leaned against the side of the buggy as if she didn't have the strength to sit upright.

Something near the front of the bakery caught his attention and he halted the mare.

"What's wrong?" Faith turned to see what he was looking at.

Through the trees, he confirmed three dark SUVs crawled along the main road as if they were looking for something...or someone.

"I've never seen those vehicles before," Eli whispered almost to himself.

Faith opened the door and started toward the buildings. Eli hopped out and hurried after her.

"What are you doing?" he asked when he caught up.

"I want to get a closer look. It could be Ghost and

his men." Her full attention was on the SUVs as they continued along.

Eli grabbed her arm. "Hang on, I'm coming with you."

Together they eased along the side of the bakery until they were close enough to see the vehicles as they passed.

"Do you recognize any of the people inside?" Eli asked once the last vehicle passed.

She shook her head, a frustrated expression on her face. "I don't, but three dark SUVs in an Amish community at one time is suspicious." She faced him. "I think those men are from New York." The weight of the world seemed to settle on her shoulders. "Are we too late?"

He tried to keep from showing his concerns. "I hope not. Let's get out of here." He reached for her hand and they ran back to the buggy.

"They're here to kill me," she said once they were moving again. She turned terrified eyes to him, and Eli's jaw tightened. He would do everything in his power to keep that from happening.

"They will deal with Vincent first."

She nodded. "We just have to keep them from finding us until the sheriff can help."

He worried that Vincent might stumble upon his *mamm*'s home once he got the truck going again. Though it was some distance from Aaron's, a determined person like Vincent would leave no house untouched. "It won't be wise for us to stay at my mother's house for long. We'll be putting Sarah and my family in jeopardy by being there. Unfortunately, Vincent knows about my place and your *grossmammi*'s. And he's been to Aaron's."

"Then where can we go? He's found us everywhere we've tried to hide."

There was only one place he could think of that would provide some amount of safety. "Miriam's *grossdaddi* had a farm that has been sitting vacant for many years. It's isolated. Toward the end of this life, he lived outside of the community. We can go there. It won't be the most pleasant place to stay, but no one should look for us there."

He fought not to show her the turmoil churning his insides. They still had a long way to go before they reached *Mamm*'s house. Now there were more dangers lurking. Men far worse than Vincent would think nothing of taking them out.

Eli hated putting his *bruder* in the line of fire, but he and Faith couldn't do this alone. He'd caused his family so much trouble in the past. Would they regret having him back?

The road they were on petered out and Eli turned back toward the main one. With sweat beading on his forehead, he headed toward his *mamm*'s home while fearing Vincent would already be there. He prayed his family and Sarah were *oke*.

Though they'd only be on the road for a short time, the exposure unsettled him. The trees had been taken down along this stretch of the road. There were a couple of vacant shops. At one time, the community had a blacksmith shop down this way, but the owner had moved away a few years ago and no one had claimed the shop since.

As Eli drew close to the former shop, he glanced

over his shoulder in time to see a vehicle top the hill behind them.

Faith noticed him looking and turned. Her attention jerked toward him. "Eli, that's them."

He had to get off the road as quickly as possible. The blacksmith's shop was the only option. The mare balked for a second under his command, confused by the sudden change of direction. She stumbled on the gravel road before regaining her footing.

"Get in the back and get out of sight," Eli urged while he guided the buggy toward the shop.

Eli stopped out front. A single SUV headed their way. Where were the others?

He turned in his seat. "Can you make it to the shop?"

Faith peeked out the back window. "I think so."

"Then hurry. It won't take the driver long to reach us. I don't know if he saw us come this way, but he might be suspicious about our sudden turn if he did. Find a place to hide and wait for me."

She opened the back door and jumped out. He watched her slip inside the building.

The SUV reached the shop. Eli hoped with all his heart that it would pass on by.

He kept his attention averted but snuck glances as the vehicle passed him. Eli blew out a huge sigh before he noticed the brake lights.

His heart stuttered as the SUV backed up. It stopped and pulled into the drive.

Please, Gott, protect us both. The prayer sped through his mind. Eli got out once the SUV stopped beside the buggy.

He waited beside the mare while the driver of the SUV exited followed by two more men.

All three were armed.

"Can I help you?" He tried to keep his tone even despite the warbling fighting in his throat. If these men had any idea of his connection to Vincent and Faith, they'd kill him in a heartbeat and take her out next. He couldn't do anything to tip them off.

"Is this your shop?" the driver asked. His accent was slightly more pronounced than Faith's.

Eli scrambled to come up with a believable response. These men would have no way of knowing the blacksmith shop was closed.

"*Jah*, it is." Eli kept his attention on the driver. The two other men walked around the buggy then started for the shop.

"I'm not open for business," Eli called out when they started to go inside.

Both men turned toward him. Their hard expressions sent a chill crawling up Eli's spine. Their attention went to the driver who motioned them back.

"That's okay, buddy, we're not looking to have our SUV fitted with horseshoes." One of the men cracked the smart remark as he passed by Eli. The second laughed along with his buddy until they got a good look at the driver. Their expressions turned sheepish.

"Sorry, boss."

Eli just wanted them out of here so he could get Faith to a safe place.

"How can I help you?" Eli asked the man in charge. The driver stuck out in the simple surroundings in his dress suit and white shirt. His dark hair was swept back from his forehead. And Eli was sure the shoes he wore cost a small fortune. The two men with him were equally attired.

"I'm looking for this man." He pulled out his phone and brought up a picture and turned it toward Eli. Not to Eli's surprise, a photo of Vincent returned his stoic expression. "Have you seen him?"

Eli shoved his hands into his pockets to keep these armed men from seeing his jitters.

"I do not think so. Why do you believe he is here? He appears to be an *Englischer*."

The man's brows rose, and his jaw hardened as if he wondered if Eli was making fun of him.

"I mean he is not Amish," Eli corrected.

"Oh, well, that doesn't matter. We have information that he's here somewhere." He stared down Eli.

Eli swallowed a couple of times. "Why are you looking for this person?"

The man's expression hardened. "That's none of your business."

Eli remained silent and the man finally added, "He works for me and I need to get in touch with him."

A lie, but Eli wasn't about to challenge it. He wanted to get rid of these men as quickly as possible.

"As I said, I do not know him." That much was true enough. He didn't really know Vincent and he didn't want to.

He pinned Eli with piercing dark eyes. "You wouldn't be lying, would you?"

Eli's heart slammed in his chest, but he kept silent.

The man's face broke into a smile. "I'm just kidding you." He brushed his finger over the phone and turned it back to Eli once more. "What about her? Have you seen her?"

Eli stared at a photo of Faith with a man he was certain was her husband.

He kept his attention on the photo as he answered. "She is not familiar either."

The man stared Eli down for a long moment before he motioned to the men to get in the SUV. He opened the driver's door and swung back to Eli. "Well, if you do see him, you'd better warn him, his boss is looking for him, and he knows why. And if you run across this woman, tell her she'd better keep moving because we're coming for her next."

The man's merciless gaze bored into Eli. He hopped inside the SUV and drove away, sending mud and slush flying in his wake.

Eli moved closer to the road while trying to stay hidden by trees. From where he stood, he saw the vehicle ease out onto the road and head back toward the shops. The driver stopped in front of the bakery. All three men got out and went inside.

While Eli was confident the young couple would not give them up to these thugs, the sooner the men left, the better.

He hurried back to the blacksmith's shop and opened the door. Faith popped up from behind a stack of firewood.

"Are they gone?" He nodded and she hurried toward him. "I was certain they'd come inside."

Eli had been, as well. "They are in the bakery now. I'm not sure how convincing I was. We should go."

Before she left the shop, he stopped her. "They had a photo of Vincent and one of you. We can't take the chance of them spotting you if they come back this way. It's best if you are out of sight until we are a safe distance away."

She nodded and he helped her up into the back of

the buggy. Eli shut the door, climbed inside and started toward his *mamm*'s home.

It felt as if they were being threatened on all sides. Eli had thought Vincent was one of the most dangerous people he'd ever met, but after his run-in with the man he believed was the drug dealer, he realized he hadn't even begun to understand the true meaning of danger.

FIFTEEN

"I don't think we were followed. It should be safe to come up here," Eli said. Even though only a small space separated them, Faith felt safer being close to him.

"These men are dangerous," she said with a relieved sigh. "They think nothing of killing people who threaten them. They won't stop until I'm dead and I'm so afraid." She faced him. "Eli, I can't let them hurt you, or my grandmother, or your family because they think you may be a threat to them, as well."

Eli squeezed her shoulder, a gentle look on his face. "Then you must do everything you can to stop them before that happens." He brushed his hand across her cheek, and she closed her eyes. Amid this nightmare, she was falling in love, and all she could think about was the danger facing them.

He spoke her name, his warm breath fanning across her face. She swallowed and opened her eyes and looked at him.

"We will get through this. *Gott* brought you back to West Kootenai for a reason. He won't let those men or Vincent have victory over you. You must believe that."

She smiled sadly. "And He brought you back, as well. He has a plan for your life too."

"I pray you are right," he said and faced forward. She could almost feel him distancing himself from her and she knew why.

"What happened to Miriam wasn't your fault, Eli. You can't blame yourself forever. Miriam wouldn't have wanted that."

A bitter laugh ripped from deep inside him. "*Nay*, she would not." His answer wasn't affirming in any way despite his agreement. "But how can I not hold myself responsible. She asked me not to go back to the logging camp. She was troubled by something that happened. I should have listened. Instead, I thought about the money I could make for us."

Her heart went out to him. "Oh, Eli, you were trying to take care of your family. She understood that."

He didn't say anything.

"Was there ever another suspect?"

"Not in the eyes of the police, but there was someone. A few days before the fire, Miriam mentioned something in passing. She said an *Englischer* had come by looking for work. She let him clean out the barn and help with feeding the animals for some wages. Miriam mentioned he'd returned again and made her feel uncomfortable. I told her I would speak with him the following week, only…"

Miriam had died.

"Did you tell the police about this man?"

He nodded. "I did. But I didn't have the man's name or a description, so they believed I'd made him up to take suspicion off myself."

Eli was doing everything he could for her, yet he'd

carried this burden of guilt for years. "If we can ask around your old community perhaps, we can find someone else who saw this man. There has to be a way."

He faced her with a bitter smile on his face. "I tried asking around, but everyone in the community had their minds made up about my guilt. They were not willing to help me."

"Oh, Eli." She reached for his hand. They might not have been willing to help, but she was going to do everything in her power to find out who killed Miriam. If she survived Vincent and the thugs he worked for, she wouldn't stop until she had answers, because if anyone deserved a second chance at happiness, it was Eli.

He glanced down at their joined hands but made no move to pull away—and she was happy about it. No matter the mountains standing between them, the doubts that kept her from trusting she could ever give her heart fully to someone else, those were problems for another day. Right now, she just wanted to sit beside this strong and courageous man and simply enjoy the feel of her hand in his.

The beauty of the mountains in the distance and the woods that surrounded the community tugged her back to a simpler time when she couldn't imagine life outside this community.

Through the years she'd told herself this wasn't her life anymore, yet everything inside her urged her to return. How different her life might have been if she'd come back sooner. There would have been more time with her precious *grossdaddi*. She could have been there for Grandmother Sarah after his passing. Married an Amish man and settled down with a family of her own. Never met Vincent.

Mamm's homestead came into view and Eli expelled a relieved sigh. Every mile they'd traveled he'd expected those dangerous men or Vincent to appear and take them out.

He kept replaying his conversation with the man he was convinced was the drug dealer. The same one who bribed New York City detectives to keep him out of jail. The person responsible for setting this terrible thing happening to Faith in motion. Dealing with such darkness was something he wasn't accustomed to and he felt ill-equipped to protect Faith from men determined to keep their crimes secret.

Letting go of his feelings of inadequacy was hard but he couldn't let them stand in the way of keeping Faith safe.

Eli stopped the buggy on top of the hill. *Mamm*'s homestead spread out below them. Almost there, yet he couldn't dismiss the feeling that something bad was coming. He scanned the countryside. Nothing appeared out of place.

He turned to Faith because he didn't trust his judgment. "Do you see anyone?"

She shielded her eyes against the morning sun and carefully surveyed the property. "No. Nothing. What troubles you?"

He couldn't explain it. "I'm not sure." Eli pulled in a breath and clicked his tongue. The mare started forward. "Vincent knows we're in this buggy." He spoke his thoughts aloud. "It will be too risky for Fletcher to use it to fetch the sheriff, which means we'll have to stay off the roads as best we can."

Faith kept her attention in front of them. "I don't understand how Blake could let someone like Vincent lead him into a life of crime he couldn't get out of. He obviously regretted what he'd done. Tried to make things right in the end. But the man I married wasn't a criminal." Her hands clenched in her lap. "Or maybe that's what he wanted me to believe. Maybe I never really knew who Blake was. All this time, I've blamed Vincent for making him into a criminal, but what if he was that way before?"

"I'm sure he loved you," Eli said, but he didn't really know much about their relationship. Faith had indicated she and Blake had been married for many years. How had Blake kept his true self hidden from her for so long? "Money can be a strong motivator." He thought about his own brush with greed. "It makes you do things you wouldn't normally do."

When she didn't answer, he looked her way. Faith's full attention was on something below.

"What is it?" He followed her line of sight. A familiar truck slowly eased along the road that ran near *Mamm*'s house. "Is that…"

"It is. It's Vincent's truck."

"How did he find us so soon?" Eli turned around the buggy and headed back into the woods while praying Vincent hadn't spotted the movement. "And how did he get those tires fixed so quickly?"

Faith continued to watch the truck's progress. "Vincent is a police officer. He probably knows who you are and where every member of your family lives." She pulled in a breath. "Blake mentioned how Vincent was paranoid about being followed. At the time, I didn't think anything of it, but now it makes sense. With everything he'd been up to, he must have had enemies everywhere." She shook her head, unable to imagine living such a life. "Blake said his brother was always heavily armed and carried tons of extra supplies wherever he went. I thought he was exaggerating, but maybe Vincent had a couple of spare tires with him."

Eli tried to recall the contents of the back of the truck where he'd found the bat. He hadn't seen extra tires, but some trucks kept them underneath the beds.

Once he had the buggy out of sight, he and Faith got out and went over to the edge of the road. The truck turned onto *Mamm*'s drive. His concern for his family escalated.

Vincent reached the house. From their vantage point, the door wasn't visible. Seconds ticked by before voices carried their way. Eli cocked his head and listened. He couldn't make out what was said but he did recognize the man speaking to Vincent. His *bruder* Fletcher.

After what sounded like a heated argument, Vincent stormed back to the truck and climbed inside. He sped down the drive and turned onto the road. Straight toward their hiding place.

Faith's posture became rigid. "He's coming toward us."

If Vincent noticed their tracks going into the woods, he'd realize someone had been there recently.

"Let's go back to the buggy." He and Faith hurried through the woods while the adrenaline spiking through his body warned they had to keep moving to live. The truck noise grew louder. Eli turned to listen. Through the trees, his worst fear came to life. Vincent had seen their tracks.

SIXTEEN

"Run!" Eli yelled and grabbed her hand. They raced toward their closing window of freedom while Faith struggled to keep fighting against the insurmountable odds facing them. She and Eli had survived some of the worst situations of their lives, yet they were nowhere close to being finished.

Gott, please, help us. We can't keep going like this.

Eli didn't waste time once they were inside the buggy. "Go, mare!" Eli slapped the reins hard and the horse jolted forward, heading back the way they'd come.

"Hey, stop!" Vincent yelled behind them. "You're not getting away this time."

There was just enough time to duck before bullets shattered the back window, flew through space and lodged in the buggy near where they were crouching. As the barrage of gunfire continued, the mare, spurred on by the danger, raced through the woods.

The shooting ended, and an eerie silence replaced it. Faith looked behind them in time to see Vincent pulling the truck into the woods. "He's coming after us!"

Their only hope was to stay in the trees and hope Vincent wouldn't be able to get the truck through.

So far, he didn't appear to have a problem. He headed straight for them.

Her stomach clenched and she watched in horror as the massive truck bounced over a downed tree without stopping.

"He won't be able to follow us through there." Eli turned hard to the right.

Eli kept the buggy moving while carefully picking his way around the trees.

She closed her eyes and prayed with all her heart for *Gott*'s protection over them.

She jerked around in her seat when a loud grinding noise sounded. Vincent had wedged the truck between two trees that appeared to be even with the doors and blocked his exit. He gunned the engine to free the truck, but it wasn't budging.

"He's stuck." She turned back to Eli, her skin tingling from shock. "Thank You, God."

Eli glanced back at Vincent who continued to spin tires, digging the vehicle into a deep rut. "He's not going anywhere for a while." He eased the buggy from the trees.

"We need my *bruders*. Without their help, we won't be able to get word to the sheriff about what's happening here, and Vincent or those other men will catch up with us. I think I can circle around behind *Mamm*'s property and come in from the back without using the road." The strain on his face confirmed they were running out of options. The longer they were out like this the more likely someone would find them.

"Do it," she said. "It's our only chance."

They traveled in silence for a while. The noise of Vincent's overworked engine faded the farther away they moved. The woods in front of them thinned into pastureland.

"We'll make better time using the pasture," Eli said when she couldn't hide her concern. "It sounds like he's still stuck. Let's hope it stays that way."

Faith's heart felt as if it were permanently installed in her throat. Her attention ping-ponged from what lay ahead to the woods they'd cleared. She expected to see Vincent emerge at any time.

Eli slowed down the mare once they reached the end of the pasture and started up an incline to the treed space separating his *mamm*'s property.

Faith's muscles tensed. Her thoughts fled in opposing directions. She couldn't get those men out of her head. "I wonder if Vincent knows they're here in West Kootenai. If he does, he'll realize his days are numbered unless he can prove himself to his boss. He's out of options." Nothing in her life, not even being a cop's wife, had prepared her for this. She couldn't imagine such evil and she never wanted to be exposed to it again.

No matter what the future held for her and Eli— whether there was a chance for them or if they were too damaged to heal—she was done with the *Englisch* ways. She'd strayed from her Plain roots, but she wanted to find her way back. Wanted to make up for all the things she should have done.

His brain swam in a fog of exhaustion. His shoulder ached. Thinking clearly was nearly impossible but he had to keep fighting. For Faith. For his family.

"Where are we?" the woman who made him want to try harder asked, and he glanced her way. She was barely hanging on, as well. He indicated the path in front of them. "These woods back up to *Mamm*'s property. We're almost there."

She managed a nod without speaking. He wished more than ever that he could take this all away for her sake. Erase it from her memory. But he couldn't.

When he looked at Faith, he saw the future that might have been. And the one he so desperately wanted, if only he was deserving of someone like her. He'd had love once and he'd messed it up terribly.

Eli gave himself a mental shake. The future was in *Gott*'s hands and he would trust Him and lean on His understanding instead of his own. Like he should have with Miriam. Until *Gott* chose to answer his prayers, Eli would do everything possible to help Faith be free of the danger following her.

The family barn appeared through the trees and his shoulders sagged with relief. Eli gave thanks to *Gott* under his breath.

"Whoa, mare." He stopped the buggy in front of the barn, the sight a welcomed one.

"Let's get it inside and out of sight. If Vincent sees it, he'll know we're connected to the house and the people here. He may try to harm my family and Sarah to force them to talk."

Eli hopped down and struggled with the door against a blustery wind that had picked up. His *bruders* must have heard the noise because Aaron and Fletcher hurried out to greet him.

"That man was here not long ago," Aaron told him. "I recognized him from the window and had Fletcher answer the door. He ranted about looking for you and Faith. He appears to be coming unglued."

Eli thought about the drug dealer Vincent worked for. With that kind of threat coming after him, Vincent was no doubt desperate to find them before this Ghost.

Once the buggy was safely inside, they left the barn. Eli told his family what happened.

"Fletcher, this is Sarah's granddaughter, Faith. You remember her from when we were *kinner*."

Fletcher nodded her way. "*Jah*, I do. I'm happy to see you again, but sorry it has to be under these circumstances." He glanced around the farm. "We should go inside. I do not trust that man not to return." They followed him to the house.

"We need your help, Fletcher. Can you use the back road and go to Eagle's Nest to bring the sheriff here?" Eli told them about what happened as the *bruders* reached the porch. "With Vincent roaming around along with those other men, I think it's too risky to use the phone shanty."

"I will be happy to help," Fletcher assured them. "I will saddle the horse and start out right away."

Eli hesitated. He didn't believe it would be safe for him and Faith to remain here for long and he told Fletcher this. "I've been thinking and the best place I can come up with for us to hide out is Miriam's *grossdaddi*'s house outside the community. No one's lived there in a long spell. I don't think those men or Vincent will look for us there."

Fletcher nodded. "A *gut* idea. I will fetch the sheriff and bring him there."

It was a small measure of relief knowing Fletcher would have help coming. *"Denki, bruder."*

They left Fletcher to saddle the horse and walked inside where the family had gathered.

Everyone turned as they entered.

"I've been so worried." Sarah hurried to her grand-daughter's side and hugged her close.

"I know, and I'm so sorry." Faith held on to her grandmother while Eli explained what they'd gone through.

Eli explained about the men from in the SUVs. "Fletcher is heading to Eagle's Nest for the sheriff. It's best if Faith and I don't stay here for long."

Details about his plan followed.

"It could take a while for Fletcher to reach the sheriff," Aaron reminded him. "Take some supplies with you."

Eli tried to pull his muddled thoughts together and agreed.

"Martha and I prepared a casserole for the midday meal," Sarah told them. "I will pack some for you to have a meal once you arrive." Together with his *mamm*, the women disappeared into the kitchen.

While the women gathered food, Aaron found a couple of flashlights along with an extra lantern and matches.

"Take *Daed*'s rifle just in case." Aaron handed Eli the weapon their *daed* had taught all the boys to shoot with.

"*Jah*. I don't know how much *gut* my shotgun will do against so many. It will be good to have extra fire-power." Eli handed Aaron back his shotgun. "Just in case," he added when Aaron would have protested.

His mother brought extra blankets to keep them

warm. They would come in handy since Eli didn't know if the house was even in usable condition.

"Denki, Mamm." Eli kissed his mother's cheek before looking to Faith. "We should go."

The family helped pack the supplies away in the buggy.

While Eli kept careful watch on the nearby road, Faith hugged her grandmother close for a long moment before she released her and got into the buggy.

Eli started to follow when Aaron stopped him. "Be careful, *bruder*. These people are far beyond anything you and I are accustomed to dealing with. Get to the house and stay out of sight. Fletcher will bring the sheriff as quickly as possible."

With Aaron's warning still ringing in his head, Eli switched horses and guided the animal toward the back of the property again.

He glanced at the woman who was settled in beside him. Faith hadn't said a word since she'd said goodbye to her grandmother. Her shoulders slumped. The guilt she carried with her was as heavy a burden as the gathering storm clouds.

He understood about the blame. He'd let it control his life. Had replayed every scenario of what-ifs in his head and they all led to him to sinking deeper into a sea of self-pity and guilt that threatened to take him under. But he didn't want to keep living that way. He wanted more. A chance to clear his name and let go of the guilt once and for all. Yet the only thing standing between him and that freedom was everything.

"I just want this to be over," Faith murmured, her tone exhausted. "I want Vincent and those other men out of my life for good."

Eli wished for the same thing. "They will be. Soon. Once the sheriff and his people know what's happening, they will take care of this. We just have to stay alive for a little while longer."

Her eyes shone with hope. "Thank you for trying so hard for me, Eli. You didn't ask for any of this when you found me at Silver Creek."

Though he couldn't explain it, what happened that night at the creek was a blessing. It had jarred him from his simple existence. Made him realize he still had breath in his body. A life to live. Happiness to find. *Gott*'s purpose to fulfill.

"I'm grateful for what happened because it brought us back together," he said. "I thought about you a lot over the years." Her expression softened. She seemed moved by his admission.

"I thought about you, as well." A whimsical smile touched her lips. "Back then, this community was my whole world. I loved everything about it."

"You can still have this life. It's possible for you to return to the Amish faith. You were but a child when you left. With time and the bishop's blessing, it's possible."

Sadness entered her eyes. "But my family moved away." The look on her face scared him.

Eli stopped the buggy abruptly. "You had no choice but to go with them, but this is your home. You are Amish." He leaned in closer. "You are Amish," he insisted.

A simple breath separated them. "I wish that were true."

"It is. It can be if you accept it." He touched his lips

to hers. No matter what the future held, he cared for her and he wanted so much for them to have a chance.

She kissed him back for a moment, then pulled away. Tears hovered in her eyes.

"What is it?"

She shook her head. Each moment that passed without her saying a word had him wondering what ugliness waited to jump out and grab him by the throat.

"You know my father forced us to leave the community?"

She had his full attention and his thoughts scattered. "I do. He and your *grossdaddi* argued. Your *daed* didn't want to be a farmer."

Her eyes turned dark and tumultuous. There was more coming. "They did argue. Toward the end it was all the time. Dad hated everything about being Amish. He finally talked my mother into leaving. I remember when they told me. I was devastated. Mom promised once we were on our own things would be different, but they weren't really." Faith tilted her head as if she were looking back in time. "No matter where we were, or what he did for a living, my father wasn't happy and it took its toll on my parents' marriage."

She pulled in an unsteady breath. "When I met Blake, I told myself things would be different between us. Even though we hadn't known each other all that long before we married, as long as we loved each other everything would be okay." A tiny smile lifted the corner of her lips. "I thought we had the perfect life."

She rubbed her hands over her arms. "And for a while, it was perfect. I loved everything about our life together." She stopped for a breath. "And then things began to change."

Eli tried to understand what her failed marriage to Blake had to do with her returning to her Amish faith, but he couldn't put the pieces together.

She waited for him to say something. When he wasn't able to bring words out, she continued. "Blake worked long hours. We rarely saw each other, and when we did, Blake didn't really talk much. I thought he wanted to spare me the horrific things he witnessed on the job." She shrugged. "I told you that I had no idea what Blake was doing, but that's not entirely true. I suspected something was wrong and I should have pressed him for answers, but I didn't. Maybe I was afraid of what he might say."

"You can't take on Blake's guilt, Faith," Eli said, and wanted her to agree. "He chose to commit those crimes, not you. And what happened between yourself and Blake doesn't mean you should shut yourself off from finding love again."

"Doesn't it? I should have seen the type of person Blake really was, but I didn't." She held his gaze. "Maybe some people are better off alone. I can't go through that again. I can't."

Eli felt as if someone had slugged him hard. "You cannot shut yourself off from finding happiness because of one mistake in judgment. Everyone makes them. Perhaps Blake wasn't the man *Gott* intended for you? You can't give up on life and happiness simply because of what happened."

More than anything, he wanted to make her see how important she'd become to him. "You are a *gut* person. With a lot to offer…someone." He'd almost said *me*. Almost given away the secrets of his heart. "And you are the first person who believed in my innocence since my family and Sarah."

Her face crumpled and she looked away. "I won't re-marry. My grandmother needs me, and I will be there for her like I should have through all these years. It's for the best this way."

It felt as if the ground had disappeared beneath his feet and he was free-falling.

From her rigid profile, he believed her mind was made up. So where did that leave them?

The answer was simple. Nowhere.

Eli kept his eyes on the road ahead while his thoughts spiraled into despair. He'd let himself have hope and it had vanished before his eyes.

From here on out, he'd do what he could to help Faith gain her freedom from Vincent and those thugs, and then he would do what he had for two years. Put one foot in front of the other and not allow himself the luxury of hope ever again.

SEVENTEEN

Her heart was breaking into a million pieces. She cared about Eli. He was a good man who deserved happiness. Would that ever be possible with her? Could she trust herself enough to love again?

Eli hadn't looked at her since she'd told him about her fears. His body language remained tense. She'd hurt him, yet every time she thought about the future, instead of seeing the possibilities of a world free of the danger chasing her, she saw a life controlled by the past. Eli deserved so much more.

The deteriorating sunny day matched her heart's gloominess.

"The weather is changing quickly," Eli said, finally breaking the silence between them. The wind continued to gust, and clouds gathered into one big mountain of a cloud. "It's unpredictable at this time of the year."

She shivered. Almost as if the weather had become a forewarning of things to come.

"Miriam used to tell me stories about her *grossdaddi*. How he changed after his *fraa* passed away. She told me Peter withdrew into himself. Whenever the family visited, it was always strained. He bought a house outside of the Amish community and let the home he and his *fraa* had shared for so long just go to waste."

"It sounds like he really loved his wife. He must have missed her a lot if he left the home they shared."

He finally smiled. "He did. I always thought it sad until I went through the same thing."

At one time, her reaction to Blake's death had been the same. She'd wondered how she would get through the pain. So much changed when she realized she had no idea who Blake really was.

What would have happened if Blake hadn't died? Would her life have continued the same way as always? With the hindsight of twenty-twenty vision, she realized the truth. She and Blake were not meant to be. If she hadn't rushed into marriage, would she have figured that out for herself?

A clap of thunder had her shrinking away. The dark clouds released their rain. Faith was grateful for the security of the enclosed buggy despite its battered state.

Eli glanced up at the sky. "We are still some ways from the house." Lightning flashed across the sky as the rain fell harder. Whipping in through the shattered back window, it soaked everything. "Let's find a spot to get out of the weather until the storm passes. There's the covered bridge over Jacob's River. It's just down from here."

Faith remembered the bridge from when she was a child. It was on a less-traveled road and had been in bad shape when she was young. She couldn't imagine what it must look like today. But if it afforded them some relief from the cold rain pouring into the battered buggy, it would be a welcomed relief.

Eli eased onto the road leading to Jacob's River.

As soon as they were out in the open, goose bumps sped up her arms. She was just being paranoid and with good reason. Still, it was hard not to be anxious when there were armed men searching for her and Eli.

Jacob's Bridge appeared in front of them through the driving rain. Even from where they were, Faith could tell it was in bad condition.

"It's been out of use for years," Eli told her when he spotted her concern. "Several years back, the county rerouted the road after building a newer bridge over the water. This bridge rarely is used anymore." He pulled the buggy onto the bridge and toward the end of the covering. Sheets of rain would make it hard to be seen should someone happen their way.

"We should be dry enough here," he said with a shrug. "Want to stretch your legs while we wait for the storm to pass?"

She did. Faith stepped down beside him.

The sad old bridge reminded her of how things changed. Nothing stayed the same. The one thing that could be counted on.

"It's a shame," she said and glanced around with a touch of sadness. "I remember how much fun it was as a little girl to travel across this bridge."

Eli looked her way and smiled. "We'd come here to fish and swim in the river. *Daed* taught all us boys how right here."

"*Grossdaddi* did me, as well." She remembered coming to the river with him often. Sometimes with her father. She smiled at the precious memories. The times when her father was happy and fun to be around.

Though rain churned up the river, there were spots

under the protection of the bridge that Faith could see through the crystal-clear water. Rocks of various colors dotted the riverbed. Fish swam through the water unaware they were being watched.

"It's beautiful here," she said. Despite the rain, a peaceful feeling permeated the area.

Eli shifted toward her. "It is." Something else was on the tip of his tongue, but the words were interrupted by the noise of squealing tires.

He and Faith whirled toward the sound. Several vehicles had stopped along the new road.

She and Eli ducked out of sight. Four vehicles—one of them was Vincent's. Though their hiding spot was secluded, if the people looked closely, the buggy might be spotted despite the rain. Faith prayed the mare would hold her peace.

While she watched, doors opened and several men emerged from SUVs. Faith edged closer to Eli. Their weapons were still in the buggy.

"What are you doing here?" Vincent's raised voice carried over the noise of the rain. The uncertainty in his tone captured Faith's full attention.

"I told you I'd give you five hours to handle the problem. You didn't. So, I will."

"I'm handling it, Ghost." Vincent almost appeared subdued. "You shouldn't be here. It's too risky."

Ghost. Hearing the name sent chills down her spine. She recognized it from the video Blake recorded. Her husband and Vincent had spoken to a man they called Ghost. This was the man she'd heard on the video. The dangerous drug dealer her husband and Vincent worked for.

Ghost's laughter drifted their way. It was a disturbing sound. "Too risky? You and your brother almost destroyed my business. I trusted you and your police minions to ensure I was insulated from the spotlight, but you've brought more upon me. Leaving this for you to handle is too risky." The man moved to within a few inches of Vincent. "Tell me why I shouldn't kill you right now and take care of the woman myself."

"Because I know where she's hiding."

Faith's troubled gaze tangled with Eli's. He shook his head as if to say that Vincent was lying. She sure hoped he was right.

"Where is she then?" Ghost asked with doubt in his tone.

Vincent hesitated. "Well, I don't know exactly where she is, but I'm closing in on her location. It's only a matter of time." He was trying to buy himself time.

"You have two hours to bring her to me. If you don't fulfill your promise this time, I'll find you, Vincent. And what you did to your brother and your wife will be nothing compared to the pain I'm going to inflict on you."

Vincent struggled to get out his words. "I'll handle it."

Ghost motioned to his men who headed back to their respective vehicles. But he wasn't ready to let go of Vincent just yet.

He jabbed his finger into Vincent's chest. "Know this. We are looking for her too. If we find her before you, then I don't need you alive. You remember I have plenty of other cops on my payroll. You helped recruit them."

With those chilling words, Ghost turned on his heel and headed back to the SUV. While Vincent stared after him in shock, the men swerved onto the road and barely missed Vincent's truck.

Faith reached for Eli's hand. Neither said a word as they watched Vincent relax. He gulped in several breaths and looked around the deserted space while rain continued to drench his clothing.

Faith ducked lower with Eli when Vincent appeared to stare in their direction.

Eli motioned toward the buggy. "Stay down low. We need to get back to the buggy to reach our weapons. Without them we are defenseless."

She swallowed before nodding. They eased toward the buggy as fast as possible in a crouched position.

They'd almost reached the back of the vehicle when the mare whinnied loudly.

Faith froze. Eli turned. His gaze slipped past her shoulder to something beyond, eyes wide and troubled.

She whirled in time to see Vincent running their way.

"Go, Eli, get to the buggy. Get away from here," she urged. But she knew he wouldn't leave her behind.

Vincent fired a shot and Faith ducked.

"Got you," Vincent murmured as he quickly closed the space between them with a smug smile on his face. He'd won in his mind, but she wasn't about to let him kill her without fighting him every step of the way.

Vincent reached her and yanked Faith to her feet. "You've caused me enough trouble." He jerked her close. "It's time to end this once and for all."

Vincent aimed the weapon at Eli. "I'll take care of him first so that you can watch him die." A gleeful expression simmered in his eyes. "I can't say that I'm going to miss you much, Faith. You always were sticking your nose where it didn't belong." He shook her roughly. "Well, look what you did to her and yourself."

Vincent held Faith in a death grip while he pointed the gun at Eli and pulled back the trigger. One of the things Blake had taught her right after they married was if someone ever tried to accost her, she was to kick and scream—do whatever was necessary—but never let the kidnapper get her into his vehicle.

Faith slammed her foot hard against Vincent's. Taken by surprise, he yelped but she didn't let up. The second blow connected with this shin. Before Vincent could react, she shoved him and he stumbled backward.

Eli sprang into motion and rammed into Vincent with full force. They stumbled along the uneven bridge. Vincent quickly lost his footing and fell to the ground.

Faith grabbed his weapon before Vincent could use it. She and Eli ran for the buggy.

Vincent sprang to his feet and started after them. They'd never make it to the buggy before he reached them.

Faith turned, planted her feet and shot the way Blake had taught her. The bullet struck Vincent's side. He screamed again and clamped his hand down on the spot.

Eli opened the buggy door. Both dove inside. Seconds later, the buggy was charging down the rough road with Vincent trying to catch them. When the buggy pulled out of Vincent's reach, he ran for the truck.

"Does the new road intersect with this one at any place?" Faith asked while watching the truck pull onto the road.

Eli shook his head. "No, unless he can find a way to

cross over the guardrail that separates the two roads.
If he does, the buggy will be no match for him. Hold
on—I'm getting off this road."

Faith grabbed the bottom on the seat as the buggy
raced down the road for a stretch.

The trees separating the two roads thinned. Vincent
had spotted them and rolled down the passenger window. The glint of the gun barrel scared the daylights
out of her. "He has another gun. Get down."

Eli doubled over just in time. A round of bullets flew
through the space where they'd been sitting.

When the shooting stopped, Faith peered over the
door. Vincent kept them in his sights while still watching the road ahead.

Eli sat up and whipped the reins to keep the mare
moving.

The two roads were separated now by only a few
trees and the guardrail.

"The old Beller place is coming up on the right.
Past it, there is pastureland and then we are no longer
in the community. Miriam's *grossdaddi*'s place is not
too far from there."

Faith kept a tight grip on the seat while Vincent appeared to look for a place to cross over.

"There's the Bellers' drive." Eli slowed the buggy
and the horse turned into the overgrown opening.

The mare galloped along, fleeing from her own
nightmare, while outcomes chased through Faith's
mind. None of them welcomed.

Their path emptied onto the homestead that hadn't
been used in years. The barn had collapsed in upon
itself and the house wasn't in much better condition.
Both passed by in a blur as the animal charged forward.

The pastureland Eli spoke of appeared in front of them. Every chance she could, Faith watched through the shattered opening in the back door. No sign of Vincent appeared yet, but she had no doubt he would circle around and come after them. They couldn't afford to slow down.

The mare tromped across the pasture, kicking up mud as she ran hard.

"There's the road." Eli pointed to a small county road. The horse struggled onto the pavement. Eli slowed their speed a bit and blew out a shaky breath, the strain on his face conveyed the turmoil they'd escaped. "I don't see Vincent or any of those other men. Thankfully, we don't have far to travel before we reach the house. Which is *gut* because it is getting dark and the rain isn't letting up."

Being caught out here in the dark wouldn't be a welcome scenario.

"When was the last time you were here?" Faith asked.

Eli waited to answer until he'd turned onto a narrow passage. "Not since I've been back in West Kootenai."

In what kind of state would they find the place once they reached the house?

With darkness closing in and the continued rainfall, cold air seeped into the buggy. Eli and Faith were soaking wet and shivering.

"We are almost there," he said as she huddled against the brisk temperature.

The drive leading to the house did little to ease her fears. It had been years since anyone had been down it.

A large shape loomed out of the darkness. Eli

brought the buggy to a halt and grabbed one of the flashlights as they got down.

He shone the light across the front of the house that appeared dark and foreboding. "Maybe it will be better on the inside."

They stepped up on the porch and muscled open the door.

Through the flashlight's beam, thick dust covered everything. Their entrance had released a cloud of it into the air. Faith coughed and covered her nose and mouth. Though it had been years since anyone had darkened the doors, at least the place hadn't been vandalized and the roof was still intact. It would keep out the turbulent weather.

"I'll carry in the supplies then get the mare out of the weather."

"I'm coming with you," she answered too quickly. The last thing she wanted was to be left alone.

Eli clasped her hand. They returned outdoors and carried in their meager supplies. Once the chore was done, he led the mare over to the barn that hadn't fared as well as the house.

It took them both pulling together to get the warped doors freed. Eli walked the mare inside. With Faith's help, they unharnessed her.

The animal hadn't eaten in many hours. Aaron had packed a bag of oats. While Eli went to the well for water, Faith dumped some of the oats into the trough and soothed the tired animal.

Once the animal was taken care of, she and Eli returned to the house.

Eli glanced longingly at the fireplace that dominated the living space. "It's too risky to start a fire."

Faith wrapped her blanket over his shoulders and grabbed a second one for herself. "That's okay." All she could think about was how much longer they had to wait before the sheriff arrived. Because her heart was ticking off every second as if it might be her last.

Eli kept close watch out the front windows and tried not to let his fears get the better of him, but it was hard. If something had happened, and Fletcher hadn't been able to reach the sheriff, they could be in serious danger.

Faith came over and handed him a plate of the casserole his *mamm* and Sarah prepared.

He smiled despite the worry in his heart. *"Denki."* He dove into the dish with relish. The simple chicken casserole, even though it was cold, had never tasted so *gut* before.

"There's water." She turned to go but he reached for her hand and held her there. Eli saw all the questions on her face.

"Just stay."

Those simple words held so much more meaning than for the moment. She nodded and took a bite from her plate.

"Do you think the sheriff is close?" she asked with her full attention and all her hope on him.

Much time had passed. His *bruder* would be careful not to take any of the more traveled roads. If all had gone well, Fletcher and the sheriff should be on their way here now. If…

"I do. It's only a matter of time now." Yet the knot in his stomach wouldn't ease. Vincent faced losing his life. It wasn't just about ending up in jail. The stakes were high.

"I hope it's soon. Eli, I'm so scared." She stared at him with troubled eyes and he reached for her hand. He loved her. There was no denying it. He wanted a future with her. Wanted her to stay and make that possible.

Eli set down their plates and tugged her closer. She went into his arms and wrapped hers around his waist.

She smelled like the outdoors he loved. A promise he wanted. Whether that promise would become a reality depended on them surviving Vincent…and her doubts.

She stared up at him and he wanted to believe that what he saw in her eyes was returned love. Was almost certain of it. He lowered his head to kiss her, but a noise outside pulled his attention away.

He let her go and opened the curtains a fraction. "Someone's coming. It must be the sheriff."

But the fear wouldn't ease.

A vehicle idled somewhere down the path. Why had they stopped before reaching the house? He couldn't think of a single scenario involving the sheriff that added up to this.

The only true explanation was…

The thought barely took life before the back door was pushed open and Vincent's menacing frame filled the door.

"He must have followed us. Seen our tracks. Run, Faith!" Eli just got the words out as Vincent lunged for him.

Before Eli could react, Vincent's hand snaked around his throat. Where was Faith?

Please keep her safe!

Eli clawed at the hands around his neck to no avail. Vincent's angry face blurred before his eyes. He was losing consciousness.

No! The word flew through his head as he fought with all his strength to be free. The world around him swam. His eyes rolled back in his head. His heart broke.

He'd let her down. She'd counted on him and he'd let her down.

EIGHTEEN

Faith ran as fast as she could across the dark space behind the house. A noise inside grabbed her attention: A loud thud. Something hit the floor hard.

Eli! No, please, no. He needed her. She couldn't think of herself over him.

Faith turned back to the house. A figure emerged from the open back door.

Vincent spotted her and leaped off the porch. She fled across the yard, running blindly, her arms pumping at her sides while rain drenched her to the core.

Each breath burned in her chest. She could hear him gaining, but she didn't dare look behind. If she could reach the trees, she had a chance of hiding from him.

Just a few more feet. But Vincent was too fast. He grabbed a handful of her hair and yanked. Faith stumbled to the ground.

He knotted his hand in her hair and hauled her up beside him. "Did you really think you could outsmart me?" The fury on his face was terrifying. "You have nothing. I have Blake's note. The hard copies. And the drive," he said with a triumphant look.

She struggled to keep from falling apart in front of him.

A smile spread over his face. "Now all I have to do is get rid of you. I already took care of him."

Her legs buckled beneath her. The thud. Eli. She loved him. Despite everything that happened with Blake, she'd fallen in love with Eli and she wanted to spend the rest of her life here in West Kootenai with him.

And now she was too late.

Tears filled her eyes. She couldn't give up. Had to keep fighting until the sheriff arrived. "You can kill me, but it won't matter. I told you, there's another file out there."

Vincent's gaze bored into her. "There is no other file." He shoved her to the ground. "You've caused me so much trouble, just like that worthless husband of yours."

She had to keep him talking until help arrived. "You killed your brother. Your own flesh and blood."

The accusation had no effect on Vincent. "You think I cared about Blake. He made a vow to me that he broke. I brought him in on what I did for my New York friends. I vouched for him. We had a sweet setup. Sure, we broke a few laws, hurt some bad people, but we were paid well for what we did. Blake could have anything he wanted."

He shook his head with disgust on his face. "And then he grew a conscience. Said he couldn't live with what we were doing any longer. He told me he was going to turn himself in. Advised me I should do the same. It would go easier on me if I did." Vincent looked at her with disbelief. "I told him, he would kill us both, but he didn't care. It was all about him again. Blake wanted out so everything had to end."

Vincent looked at her without seeing her. "Cheryl had her suspicions through the years, but she never said anything. I knew how to keep her in line until you called her that day," he seethed. "There was something different about her when she confronted me with what was on those pages. It was as if I'd lost control. I knew she had to die." He finally focused on Faith. "Just like you. I have to make things right with him. I'm not dying for that worthless husband of yours. And I'm certainly not dying for you."

Eli's eyes shot open. He coughed and sputtered as he struggled for air. Pulled in a dozen breaths. Faith. She was in danger.

He stumbled to his feet. The house was empty. She was gone.

Fear spiraled through him. He searched for his weapon, but it was gone. Vincent must have taken it. Eli ran out the open door.

The rain plastered his hair against his head. He had no idea where Vincent had taken her. Eli forced himself to stop and listen.

Off to the left, someone was yelling. Vincent!

He ran toward the sound. As the man's voice grew louder, Eli stopped when he reached the edge of the woods. Peering through the deluge, he spotted them. Vincent stood over Faith, the gun inches away.

Eli charged Vincent. The man heard him coming a tick before Eli slammed into his frame.

Despite being injured and losing blood, Vincent fought with the strength of someone who had every-

thing to lose. As they scuffled, Vincent put the handgun into position and fired. The bullet sliced across
the same arm that Vincent had shot before. Eli grabbed
the injured limb while Vincent prepared to shoot him
again.

He couldn't let this man win. He had too much to
lose. Eli grabbed for the gun. The shot ripped through
the air close to his ear, temporarily taking away his
hearing.

But Eli didn't give up. He fought with a strength he
didn't know he possessed. With everything he could
muster, he slugged Vincent. The blow landed. Vincent's
head shot sideways, then his eyes slammed shut and
he crumpled to the ground.

Relief and spent adrenaline weakened Eli's knees,
and he dropped to them.

Faith rushed to Eli's side. "Are you okay? He shot
you."

"It is not so bad." Eli played down the pain in his
arm. She helped him to his feet. He had to find a way
to restrain Vincent until the sheriff arrived. Eli didn't
want him getting away again. It was time for Vincent to pay for the terrible things he'd done. A set of
handcuffs was attached to the man's belt. Eli removed
them and with Faith's help, they dragged Vincent to
a nearby tree. Eli secured Vincent's hands around the
trunk with the cuffs.

Eli found the key to the cuffs in Vincent's pocket
and searched for any other weapons. Inside one pocket
he found something far more important—the drive
Faith had been searching for.

All he could think about was he'd almost lost her.
Eli gathered her into his arms. Facing death made him

realize how much he cared for her. How much he loved her. She'd brought him back to life when he didn't believe it possible. Would she trust him enough for him to prove he'd be at her side no matter what the future brought?

"*Komm*, let's get out of the weather." With his arm around her waist, they headed back to the house.

As they neared the structure, strobing lights approached the abandoned farm. Fletcher had brought help and plenty of it.

The sheriff had arrived along with several of his men and EMTs.

Sheriff Collins and Eli's *bruders* approached where he and Faith waited.

"There's a man restrained to a tree through there." Eli pointed toward where they'd left Vincent.

The sheriff motioned to two of his men who went after Vincent.

"Looks like you have a couple of nasty injuries." The sheriff nodded toward Eli's arm. "Let the EMTs have a look at it before I get your statement."

Faith waited beside the sheriff while Eli was treated for his wounds.

With everything that happened, he'd almost forgotten the drive. He pulled it out and handed it to the sheriff. "Everything you need to convict Vincent St. Clair should be on this, but you should know there are some men from New York out there looking for Faith as well."

"You found it," Faith said in surprise and Eli nodded.

"I did. Vincent had it tucked in his pocket."

The sheriff tipped back his hat. "Not anymore

they're not. We picked up half a dozen men earlier. I ran their names. Most have outstanding warrants in New York. One of them, Isaac Hamilton, goes by the street name of Ghost. There have been more than a dozen murders associated with him. No one's been able to make any of them stick." The sheriff examined the drive. "It appears salvageable."

"There's a video on it showing Vincent and my late husband along with one of the men you have in custody," Faith told the sheriff. "Ghost. They are discussing a drug deal." Faith managed a brief smile as she finished. The days of being on the run had taken their toll on her.

Sheriff Collins held up the drive. "It sounds as if it will help. Along with both of your testimonies, we should have enough to get these men off the streets. Maybe we can convince one of them to turn on the others and we can convict the rest of the dirty cops."

Faith looked to Eli for support before she gathered a breath and told the sheriff about Cheryl's death.

Once she'd finished, Sheriff Collins shook his head. "I have no knowledge of you being wanted for her murder, but I'll check with New York. I think once St. Clair sees the evidence against him, he'll back off on the claim you killed his wife. It will be better for him if he cooperates and helps us put away the man he's been working for."

The sheriff's gaze shifted to where his men brought out Vincent. "Excuse me," he said and headed that way.

Once it was the two of them, Eli looked into Faith's eyes. It was as if the weight of the world had been freed from her shoulders and he was so happy for her. He loved her and wanted to be there for her through all of life's ups and downs. But would his love be enough to convince her not to live in fear any longer? He wanted to take that chance.

He clasped her hand and drew her closer. Wanted to clearly see her face when he told her how he felt about her.

"I love you, Faith, and I want to spend the rest of my life with you." He stopped just for a second to collect his thoughts. He wanted to say this right. "I never thought it would be possible to feel this way again, but you've made it possible. You make me feel alive again."

Tears filled her eyes, yet she remained silent.

"I know you've been through a lot and you said you would never remarry, but I'm asking you to trust me not to be like Blake. Trust me to be at your side no matter what goes wrong. Trust me to be the man you need me to be. I love you, Faith, and it doesn't matter to me what the future holds as long as I have you."

He waited. Uncertain of what she would say until she smiled. And all his fears evaporated.

He brought her into his arms and kissed her with all the love overflowing inside his heart.

"I love you too, Eli. And I want to spend the rest of my life with you here in West Kootenai."

"No matter what?" he asked because he had to be sure he wouldn't lose her again.

She smiled with all her heart. "No matter what."

He kissed her again and marveled at the love that had come from so much heartache. He held her tightly and realized, no matter what the future held, as long as they had *Gott* and each other, they'd weather every storm that came their way.

EPILOGUE

One year later...

The sound of a vehicle approaching caught Faith's attention and she hurried to the front window.

She had never imagined her life could be so happy until she married Eli. Being his *fraa* had made her realize what she had with Blake had been an illusion. This love—this life they had built here in West Kootenai—was real.

A sheriff's patrol slowly eased down the path toward the house. Faith wiped her hands on her apron and stepped out to meet the man who had become her and Eli's *gut* friend.

Sheriff Collins and many of his people had attended Faith and Eli's wedding six months ago.

After arresting Vincent and Ghost and his men, Sheriff Collins had kept them apprised of what was happening. She and Eli had given their statements and were prepared to testify once the trial began, but Vincent had worked out a deal where he would serve out his sentence in a prison away from Ghost and his people. In exchange for the deal, Vincent provided information that would put the other criminals away for a very long time. He'd rolled on his former boss and his fellow cops. She and Eli would not have to appear at the trial. For that she was relieved. If she never saw Vincent again, it would be too soon.

Faith realized the approaching vehicle belonged to Sheriff Collins.

Eli must have heard the noise, as well. He came from the barn to join her on the porch. Her husband wrapped his arm around her waist and tugged her close as Sheriff Collins got out and waved before heading their way.

"Good to see you both," he said in his usual friendly way. "I came because I have news for you, Eli."

Eli's gaze shot to her. "What kind of news?" She could feel her *mann*'s tension growing. Eli had been living under the cloud of his past far too long and she so wanted to free him.

Sheriff Collins was smiling, so Faith was certain it was not bad news. "I just got off the phone from the chief of police in Libby." He stopped and watched them both before adding, "They found the person who killed Miriam."

Though Faith had prayed for this moment for a long time, she still couldn't believe it was happening.

"Would you like to come inside for some *kaffe*?" she asked, and the sheriff agreed.

She poured three cups, placed one in front of the sheriff and waited.

"The man who killed Miriam is named Henry Langston, a local Libby man." The sheriff looked to Eli for recognition.

Eli shook his head. "I don't know the name."

Sheriff Collins nodded. "I'm not surprised. He kept

to himself a lot. But apparently, he was going through some hard times and was doing odd jobs around the community. He'd asked Miriam if she could use some help. Langston said she let him do a few chores around the place. Apparently, he became infatuated with her." The sheriff waited for Eli to say something, but he stared at the sheriff, unable to speak.

"Anyway, Langston broke into another house and killed the owner. He tried to set a fire to cover up the crime, but the homeowner had an alarm system so the Libby police caught him before he was able to cover up his crimes. The similarities between this murder and Miriam's death were enough to make the chief question the man further. He eventually confessed to killing Miriam."

Faith watched Eli. What the sheriff said matched what he'd told her before.

"On the night of the fire, he went to the house and told her he loved her. She tried to shut the door on him, but he forced his way in. When she ran, he choked her unconscious and then set the fire to cover the crime."

Faith grabbed Eli's hand and squeezed it. Her husband stared at the table, swallowing several times.

"I can't believe it. Miriam never mentioned his name. A man whose name I didn't know took her life."

"I know you feel guilty about not being there to save her," Sheriff Collins said. "But you can't hold on to that guilt, Eli. You have too many blessings to keep it in your life." He looked to Faith and smiled. The sheriff finished his coffee and rose. "I should be on my way. I just wanted to let you know, you are clear of any suspicion. Live your life in the now and in the future, Eli. Don't look back."

They followed the sheriff out onto the porch and waved as he headed to his cruiser.

Once he'd gone, Faith put her arm around her husband's waist. "I'm sorry that Miriam had to die like that, but this proves it wasn't your fault."

Eli stared into her eyes. "It's still hard. I feel I let her down by being obsessed by making money, but Miriam wouldn't want me to hold on to the past. And the sheriff is right. I am truly blessed because I have you."

And so was she.

Eli leaned down and kissed her tenderly and she placed her hands on his face, keeping him there.

"I love you," she said with all her heart. "More than anything, I love you, and I'm so glad I found you."

As he looked into her eyes, he slowly smiled. "And I love you, too, my beautiful *fraa*. You have made me happier than I ever thought possible, and I look forward to every moment of my life together with you."

A happiness Faith never thought possible again filled her heart. This was where she'd belonged all her life. The place she'd been searching for even when she didn't realize it. This was home. And she'd never leave it, or Eli, again.

* * * * *

If you enjoyed this story, don't miss Mary Alford's next Amish romantic suspense, available later this year from Love Inspired Suspense!

Find more great reads at www.LoveInspired.com

Dear Reader,

Sometimes, the hardest part of letting go of the past is forgiving yourself for the mistakes you've made. If you let them, mistakes can keep you from realizing the blessings God has in store for you.

Shielding the Amish Witness is a story about the journey of two people weighted down by mistakes and running from their pasts. When a chance meeting reunites two former childhood friends, they not only find the redemption they have been searching for, but also a second chance at love. All because they let go of the past and embraced the future God had in store for them.

I so hope you enjoy Eli and Faith's journey from broken to forgiven, and I hope their second-chance story inspires you to find your own.

God Bless,
Mary Alford

Lex Fielding drove, cutting down the narrow dirt path
between the towering trees. Branches slapped the side
of his park-ranger truck, and rocks spun beneath his
wheels. All the while, words cascaded through his mind,
clattering and colliding in a mass of disjointed ideas that
didn't even begin to come close to what he wanted to
say to Poppy. Years ago, he'd had no clue how to explain
to the most incredible woman he'd ever known that he
didn't think he was ready to get married and have a
family. He might not have even had the guts to tell her all
his doubts, if she hadn't called him out on it after he'd left
a really unfortunate and accidental pocket-dial message
on Poppy's voice mail admitting he wasn't ready to get
married.

Something about being around Poppy had always made
him feel like a better man than he had any right being.
Even standing beside her made him feel an inch taller.

He just hadn't thought he'd been cut out to be anyone's husband. Something he'd then proved a couple of years later by marrying the wrong woman and surviving a couple of unhappy years together before she'd tragically died in a car crash.

He heard the chaos ahead before he could even see it through the thick forest. A dog was barking furiously, voices were shouting, and above it all was a loud and relentless banging sound, like something was trying to break down one of the cabins from the inside.

He whispered a prayer and asked God for wisdom. Hadn't been big on prayer outside of church on Sundays back when he'd been planning on marrying Poppy. But ever since Danny had been born, he'd been relying on it more and more to get through the day.

Then the trees parted, just in time for him to see the two figures directly in front of him dragging something across the road. His heart stopped.

Not something. *Someone.*

They had Poppy.

Don't miss
Wilderness Defender *by Maggie K. Black,*
available May 2021 wherever Love Inspired Suspense
books and ebooks are sold.

LoveInspired.com

LISEXP0421